The Harder Right

THE HARDER RIGHT

STORIES OF CONSCIENCE AND CHOICE

Arthur Dobrin

Print ISBN: 978-0-7867-5526-4
ebook ISBN: 978-0-7867-5527-1

Distributed by Argo Navis Author Services

CONTENTS

INTRODUCTION

I'M PASSIONATELY CONCERNED ABOUT HOW PEOPLE
live and how to make the world a better place. For more than
thirty years I was the Leader of the Ethical Humanist Society of
Long Island, an organization dedicated to living an ethical life.
And when I retired from that post, I taught courses in applied
ethics at Hofstra University. I also was trained at the Ackerman
Family Institute as a family psychotherapist.

Throughout my multiple careers I've written about philosophy, social psychology and moral education, but I've also published poetry and fiction and have written plays. All are aimed at
the same things—making people more aware, thoughtful, sensitive and responsible.

I am convinced that people are happiest when they lead virtuous lives. But still I am nagged by questions. What is it that makes
people moral? What is it that people are really after, and what do
they want out of their lives? What motivates people?

As the Leader of the Ethical Humanist Society, I worked with adults and children, helping sort through the often murky mess that life is and figuring out what to do about complicated and conflicted situations. As a university teacher, I've tried to find the best way to influence my students to become better people. And as a therapist I tried to understand what motivated people to do what they do.

In all three roles I came to realize that there is no one right way to live; seldom are there clear-cut answers about what is the right thing to do. I also learned that some approaches to life are better than others. Sometimes what helps shed light is philosophical, even abstract, where concepts are used to illuminate difficult situations. Other times, the approach is indirect, where literature serves better than philosophy. Sometimes an insight makes the difference.

The Harder Right is a collection of short stories designed to stimulate discussion about ethical situations. The stories themselves do not judge the characters or present solutions to the situations they face. That is left to the reader. These stories can be enjoyed simply as they are or they can provide grist for discussions. I have used them in graduate and undergraduate business ethics classes and in a required media ethics class for undergraduate communications majors at my university. I have also led discussions based on the stories for adults in libraries.

Empathy and stories: educating the heart

Historian Lynn Hunt, in her book *Inventing Human Rights*, links human rights to the reading of novels. The idea of civil rights had been around for a while but it wasn't until the 18th century, she says, when the modern novel evolved, that moral concerns, which had been restricted to white, propertied males, extended to all people. The novel and human rights arose in tandem.

People have a natural sympathy for those around them. Literature's great contribution to the moral enterprise is that it provided the psychological groundwork for people to care about others who were not part of their circles of family and kin. Readers entered into unknown worlds in their own homes and in the privacy of their own space. Their compassion was spurred to include those who they didn't know and who were dissimilar.

Readers imaginatively entered into the lives of servants and slaves, rich and poor, farmers and city dwellers, the powerful and the desperate.

Emotional involvement with fictional characters first pushed people to recognize the rights of everyone; philosophical arguments clinched the deal. Readers were moved by the lives of people (fictional as they were) whose worlds they entered through the stories that unfolded slowly, over days on the page. A reader felt another's joy, suffered along with another's grief, and felt what it was like to make difficult choices that they themselves may never have faced. By expanding the inner lives of the reader, their circles of concern grew to encompass different groups of people.

For the first time, the ruling class understood the inner lives of others who were unlike themselves. Now everyone, regardless of class, sex or race, was viewed as human. Outward differences began to fade away as insignificant as the inner lives became more vivid.

Novels widened the circle of the human family, Hunt argues. I don't know if her argument is historically accurate, but I do know that the insight that she presents regarding the power of literature

is correct. A necessary part of being moral is the ability to identify with another person and that is exactly what good stories do.
Psychologists call this 'perspective taking'; you place yourself in
another's shoes and because of this you now take their interests
seriously. When, through reading, you take on the perspective of
strangers, the moral circle is enlarged.

Critical thinking and stories: educating the mind

Making connections with others is a necessary part of ethics. But
it isn't always sufficient. Ethics also entails judging. This is the
capacity to distinguish right from wrong and good from bad,
knowing what one ought to do and what one should refrain from
doing. Judging is evaluating a situation or another person's character and ranking the alternative choices. Appraising someone or
some situation is to say that one thing is more important than
another. Empathy and compassion are necessary, but deciding
between competing notions of what to do is also required, especially when matters are complex or there are conflicting values.

Imaginative literature is a good vehicle for the emotional com-
ponent of morality, and it can also help with ethical judgments
when the stories themselves are thought provoking. A story that
is conflict free doesn't facilitate judgment but merely reinforces
the reader's preconceived ideas, especially about what is right and
wrong. Rather than fostering independent thought, such stories
are moralistic. Stories that end with, "The moral of the story is. . .
." address an elementary level of morality, when children are learning social rules. But for more mature readers, stories with obvious
morals aren't very helpful in developing practical wisdom, since
moral decision-making requires complex and critical thought.

Following rules and judging what is right and wrong or good and bad are distinct undertakings. A computer can be programmed to provide correct answers regarding rules but no program can substitute for good judgment or decide which moral values are more important than others.

About the stories

Reading can educate the heart and the mind. So these stories can be enjoyed the same way you might any other collection. But there is even more to be gained when there is group discussion. Dialogue is a useful means of gaining new insights. Listening to others—and knowing what you think by listening to yourself speak out loud—continues to deepen your insight and appreciation.

A discussion guide is presented at the end of the book, as are the inspiration and sources of many of the stories.

The Harder Right consists of mash-ups of news items, stories from real accounts that I am familiar with from my roles as Leader of the Ethical Humanist Society of Long Island and marital therapist, and as a university teacher. A few stories incorporate "thought experiments" that are much discussed by ethical philosophers.

"Passing Stranger" relates the story of a religious leader whose decision ostracizes her from her colleagues and congregants. The next two stories, "Love the One You're With" and "Lemon" share the theme of adoption and raise questions about love and loyalty. "Shila" is a girl who follows her conscience so scrupulously that the line between principles and insanity is questioned.

"Kartik's Last Letter" is an account of an immigrant who writes to his sister about his life in the United States and presents something less than the truth about his situation, while Melita, in "Girls in Paradise" has to confront her feelings about protecting her own integrity or helping the girls she is pledged to support.

The beginning of the Nazi era provides the backdrop to "The Train to Amsterdam," as the Altman family makes momentous decisions about their future, not knowing what the reader does about the coming years. A similar dilemma is presented in "Black Ice," as a rebellious daughter struggles for personal independence at the same time that her ethnic group becomes the object of vicious attacks.

"(E)ruction (D)isorder" is a humorous view of the allure of money. "Coral Fish" is a science and philosophical fantasy about a society that makes no distinction between feelings and behavior.

What secret can be so deep that people are willing to give up the life they know in order to keep it? This is presented next in "In Treasured Teapots."

The last two stories have military settings. In "Deep Well," Kent, a conscientious cadet, is faced with putting his own future on the line in order to live up to his principles, and in "The Harder Right" Jason deals with making a choice between the lesser of two evils that first presented itself to him in a dream.

PASSING STRANGER

A WOMAN.

Perhaps that's why.

The first—and still the only one—in the clergy association.

Or maybe it is because of where she is from.

No one from San Francisco had come to live here before. Occasionally an outsider moved to this town, in the northern tier of the state, but the flow is almost always in the other direction, away from, not into. And the few who do come to stay aren't from California, a place that to this day, decades after hippies became homeowners and Social Security recipients, is believed to be an incubator for radical lifestyles and subversive politics.

Or perhaps her name—Ailanthus—a strange one, where here, if you are named after flora it is Rose or Violet or another sweet smelling flower that could be grown in the garden. It must be a name given to her by a hippie mother, a band given to bestowing peculiar names on their children. No one knows of a girl being named after a tree. They never heard of an ailanthus before she

7

arrived; they certainly never saw one growing in this land where trees are conifers and hardwoods. But her mother, from Brooklyn, had seen many sprouting in unexpected places and thought them beautiful, with clusters of yellowish flowers that turn rust red throughout the seasons, the tree growing where no other would take root. When they discovered that Ali was her shortened name and learned what her given, formal name was, a few thought that if she were going to be named after a tree, it should be Pine. She heard it before, as a schoolgirl, sometimes as a taunt, other times spoken affectionately. She knew all the variations, such as Ice Cream and Traffic. An athletic friend gave her the pet name, which she liked, Soccer.

Tree-of-heaven is its common name, a good one from parents who thanked God for delivering a child, a good name, she thought, when she became a woman and found herself in this career. And the tree is an appropriate metaphor for those who harbor malicious thoughts but won't speak them to anyone except behind closed doors—an invasive species, a threat to natives, insidiously taking root where it doesn't belong. If her mother knew that the scent of the male flowers resembled cat urine, would she have given her that name? It never occurred to Ali to ask until now.

Being single also raised suspicions.

Unmarried, thick black hair that cascades like rivulets to her dark neck, a pleasing round face with soft gray eyes, never having been married, at least according to the story she chooses to tell—in her early thirties, affable, restrained and with a voice as beautiful as the best in any church choir. Chaste? No one asks the other question, but speculation circulates: wasn't it in San Francisco that one of "them" became a minister and isn't that the city where there is a congregation just for those like that? Does she even own a dress? And her expensive cowboy boots that she wears for all occasions, how can you explain that?

Like a priest, she said with a smile when first asked by one of the pastors in the association about her not having a spouse, not realizing that her response raised hackles for a different reason. Later she reccognized the clumsiness of her quip. There isn't a Catholic church for miles and the local university, the largest private college in the county, only recently removed from its website a denunciation of "false Catholic doctrine" and how one could not "be a good Catholic and a good, spiritual Christian." At first, some did think that maybe for her it was also a religious requirement, but that misconception was quickly dispelled after the meeting, about a year after her appointment to the congregation and she joined the Buffalo County Clergy Association, when she was asked to present a short lecture at one of the monthly meetings.

"I am a cantor," she said, explaining that her training was slightly different than that of a rabbi's but was authorized to perform and carry out all the same religious duties. A rabbi was a teacher, the most learned in the community, she said, happy to enlighten her more insular colleagues; as a cantor she was the leader of congregational prayers, prayers always sung in the Jewish tradition. As a professional cantor, having graduated with a degree in Master of Sacred Music and receiving investiture as Cantor from the seminary, she was ordained clergy and it was not unusual in these circumstances for a congregation to employ a cantor instead of a rabbi.

"I am the leader of the congregation," she said.

Of the Tamarack Jewish Center, an aspirational name for a group that rented space from The Benevolent and Protective Order of the Elks.

"Just like all of you are in yours. I officiate at weddings, tend to the sick and preside at funerals. I am their clergyperson."

A strange locution but most got used to it and if she wanted to refer to herself this way, that was fine with most.

Other questions: No, her father didn't dress in black and wear a long beard. (At least not since college.) We are from the liberal branch of Judaism, she said. No, I don't mind that you serve ham sandwiches after our meetings. I don't eat lobster, though. We never ate it in my family. We didn't keep kosher in my family; not even my grandparents. But just in case the kosher laws are immutable and He's watching, you know, this is the one food that if he found me eating, He would strike me dead.

Yes, it is true, there are Jews who won't drive on Saturday, do any work, including cooking or turning on electric lights, or touch money on the Sabbath, she said in response to an Evangelical minister who led a trip to Israel and had seen some of these things with his own eyes, but Reform Jews don't abide by those rules. No one dared ask her if it was true—'I heard . . .'—that Jews had intercourse through a hole in the bed sheet. But how would she know about that anyway? Having sex on the Sabbath was considered a blessing, she said at one meeting, when there was consternation about sexualized contemporary life. Even if you aren't married? no one dared ask, but if someone had, she would have waved it off with a joke. She had lots of jokes, most of which she never related to the Buffalo County Ministers Association, many of which, though, she told to her congregants over a dinner at their homes.

Everyone agreed that Rabbi Ali, as she was universally known despite her disclaimer, had a wonderfully self-deprecating sense of humor. It served her well in fending off Rev. Tyler who was glad to have the chance to meet a Jew, a person he tried to bring into the warm arms of Jesus or those who, in charming innocence, tried to set her up with an eligible bachelor. Of which there were none at the Jewish Center. All those who were single would make good companions for her widowed mother in Boca Raton.

A Jew, most of all.

Although, if anything, her fellow clergy had been too solicitous towards her, exhibiting a genial condescension, even an effusiveness by the pastor calling himself a Christian Zionist, accepting her membership into their association as if proving their Christian magnanimity. But now, for some, her religion was enough to prove the point that they had been mistaken, even though the charge, brought and debated at a meeting where Ali was asked to leave when the vote was taken was couched as "behavior unbecoming a minister," as reported in the minutes, without names attached to positions or the final tally listed. Expulsion edged out censure. 'Money grubbing' was uttered off the record, in a phone call, on a walk to the car in the church parking lot. But the main motivation couldn't be that since the Jewish Center, too, was split, with as many detractors as supporters, often expressing the same outrage. When the matter became public, making a brief appearance in the national news, Ali knew that she had to leave Tamarack, Buffalo County.

*L*eading a religious community, spending her life as a religious leader, came unplanned, as much a surprise to her as it was to her parents, who, while expecting something unconventional from their daughter, found this calling and the place to which it took her startling. Music, not religion, was her passion. She had piano and voice lessons, she performed in every school musical, spent her money on records and concerts. She wanted to be Madonna. She listed to Barbra Streisand. She started her own grunge band and learned arias from Kathleen Battle. She imitated Liza Minnelli and was happy when she could buy a CD version of Cabaret because her LP of the show was too scratched to listen to.

Countless songs lurked in her head and she never knew silence or stillness. She churned with melodies and lyrics. Ali was always singing to herself; songs became vocal when prompted by random events, a sight, a sign, an overheard conversation, phrases from dialogues with friends, a recalled memory. As the controversy in Tamarack erupted, she found herself singing "Money makes the world go round, the world go round," and she thought about being a Jew in a Christian world, where it wasn't whether you believed in Jesus but which church you attended and the Jewish bible was treated like an embarrassing relative, a crazy uncle locked in the attic. She hadn't known these waters before moving here. For Ali, being Jewish was simply one of many identities that she carried; she came from places so heterogeneous that being different was taken for granted.

Ali's immersion in music led her to the Berklee College of Music, in Boston, where she majored in Performance, did summer stock in the Berkshires, and, after graduation, performed in a variety of plays, musicals and legitimate theater, in troupes Off Broadway and in Los Angeles, where she was seduced into settling, hoping to parlay her small part in a big musical film—which one reviewer said she was the only breath of fresh air in an otherwise stinker of a movie—into a screen career. While waiting, she did voice-overs for TV commercials, worked as a singing waitress and played the back-up banjo on the CD of a pop singer from Finland that, when the album became the indie hit of the year, gave her just enough money and hope for a year to alleviate a bout of melancholic gloom.

In Los Angeles Ali missed the urbanity of New York and Boston, the ability to get places without a car, the gray skies of cold, damp days and the flaming leaves of autumn. She slowly closed in on herself and spent more time reading. She took up yoga for six month, registered for an art class, and tried meditating. But the solitariness was more than she wanted. As she became more introspective, she also wanted to extend herself, not with companionship but with giving. What really compelled her to perform, she discovered, was what it brought to other people. While she needed approbation and craved attention, the audience needed her just as much.

One Friday night, after reading an ad in a local newspaper, out of boredom and curiosity, she went to the Creative Arts Temple, where, along with a congregation of mainly young singles and couples, she sang, clapped, laughed and listened to a sermon that moved her to tears. As she wrote on her application to the cantorial school in San Francisco, "God took me by the hand and brought me through the doors of heaven." This struck the admissions committee as being a little too Christian in its language, but, after some discussion, chose to interpret her remarks as aesthetical.

"But you've never been religious before. Why now?" she was asked at the interview.

"I've always been religious—spiritual—I just didn't know it, but that's what music has been. I've always been moved by the human voice, but nothing like the way the sacred music of the temple touched me. I now know how important it is being a Jew, to be a Jew, when I went to the temple in LA for the first time. I now go every Friday night. If possible. It's important for me to support the cause of the Jewish people. I don't know what else to say, how to explain it."

As a rabbi, she would need to be more articulate—a teacher, a scholar, a spokesperson on behalf of the congregation to the larger community, an organizer, a comforter to the sick and bereaved. As a cantor, the beauty of her voice and command of the liturgical music would be sufficient. Ali's desire to use her talent to serve the Jewish community grew deeper with each course at the school, her appreciation for Jewish heritage deepening, and she was never more certain that she had made the right decision by the time she graduated.

*F*inding a position as a cantor was more difficult than had been getting work in the theater. Large synagogues wanted an experienced cantor to assist a senior rabbi, while small synagogues wanted a rabbi, not a cantor, to lead the congregation. Ali had reconciled herself to remaining a congregant when she learned that a group in the Plains States, one that rented space in an Elks Hall on Friday nights, had received a sizeable grant from a member whose software company made him a millionaire when it went public, hoped that with the help of a professional, they could grow into a full-size congregation.

"Do you really want to go to such a God forsaken place, Ali?" her mother asked.

"Nowhere is forsaken by God," she answered with humor.

"Are there really Jews there?"

"Enough to pay me a half-time salary."

"And the other half?"

"The person who gave the endowment has connections," she said. "He arranged for me to teach music part-time at a community college, about an hour's drive away. There are a few private colleges around. So I might be able to get another class. And giving music lessons. That's enough for me to get by."

That part was easy, the money, having more than enough to get by. The hard parts were: no balsamic vinegar or kettle potato chips or authentic Italian sauce, craft beer or Napa wines—she lived long enough in northern California to have become a foodie; there being no other single Jew her age for her to talk to in person; the brutal winter cold and her not liking snow shoeing. However, she surprised even herself, for not only did Ali perform all her pastoral duties well, as the only clergy for the congregation, she found great pleasure in it—the advice sought after by members more than twice her age, the comfort she gave to those in need, the confessional secrets she kept locked away.

She grew accustomed to these deprivations and found the newborn meaning in her life more than compensation. Not being able to reverse the diminishing number of congregants—that was dispiriting but also challenging. Despite the unlimited funds provided by the benefactor, membership never exceeded fifty. Sometimes more guests attended than members. Only when there was a wedding or bar mitzvah or funeral did the Elk's Hall fill to capacity and it looked as though the Tamarack Jewish Center might have a future.

When her first contract expired, after two years, the board voted to retain her and offered her lifetime tenure, the funding assured by the benefactor.

"No," she countered, "five years." And negotiated a full-time salary "so I won't have to divide my attention. If I can't build the congregation by then, then I'm the wrong person. You need someone else."

Members were scattered as far as one hundred fifty miles from Tamarack—a horse farmer, a social worker, a mining company manager, the director of a lumber mill, store owners, teachers, secretaries, a doctor, an accountant, a real estate agent, a mechanic, an extension agent on an Indian reservation, an organizer with the Farmers Union, retirees, four children. The reality was that Tamarack Jewish Center couldn't grow without a new influx of Jews into this part of the state, an unlikely prospect, although not completely impossible, as the conversion of a declining meat packing plant in Postville, Iowa, into a kosher meat slaughtering company showed how a community could be revived and transformed in a few years.

When Ali talked about her struggle to keep the Center going, the minister of the New Life Bible Church offered to give her materials that he had used on how to build a congregation. His was a successful mission with a new church with theater-style seating; several Sunday services were held to accommodate the thousands of worshippers. Ali read the books he gave her and everything she could about congregation building. At her urging, TJC hired a consultant for three days, an expert in taking small congregations and expanding them to what they called "full-service congregations." Her board then sent Ali for in-depth training at the interfaith Alban Institute.

Her diligence, her competence and charisma didn't matter. All the right tools with all the right experts still need the proper materials and this was lacking. No new industry came to Tamarack, no failing company was infused with fresh cash and Ali's optimism continued to be only her public face. And this she could no longer maintain when a family, with the bat mitzvah girl in the van, died in a road accident on the way to the service. Shortly after, another congregant died a painful death from melanoma.

*T*he phone call couldn't have come at a worse time for Ali. "Rabbi Cohen," the caller asked. She didn't bother to correct him.

"Who is this?" she asked. She couldn't bring herself to put on her professional voice. She responded as though this were a solicitation from an unwanted charity.

"My father died. I'm calling from Chicago."

"My condolences," she said. She breathed deeply and sat down on the high stool next to the kitchen counter. "I'm sorry. And who am I speaking to?"

He told her. "But what was your father's name?"

The caller explained.

"My father lived in Grange."

"Grange?" she said. She had driven through the small town a few times, on the way to a clergy retreat. "I know where that is.

That's not too far from here." She searched her memory. "Did he just move to the state? I'm sorry I don't know your father."

"No," the caller said. "He's been here for quite a while. Twenty years about."

Ali hesitated. She found herself bothered by not knowing about him. She didn't know there were Jews in Grange. "How could I not know him? I think I must know every Jew within two hundred miles of here."

"He wasn't a joiner."

Ali spoke calmly as she took a pencil from the holder and began to take notes for the service. "You mean that he was a loner?"

"No, he was actually a social person," the son said. "If you ask anyone in Grange, they'll tell you how much they liked him. He was president of The Rotary and I'm pretty sure he was also president of the Chamber of Commerce."

"I don't understand," Ali said. "How is it that I've never met him? He's not associated with the Center. How is it that don't I know him?" She put down her pencil. She sensed the answer and didn't like it.

"He wasn't a joiner. About religion, I mean. He didn't like organized religion."

Ali pushed her chair aside and before she thought about what she wanted to say, she blurted, "Then why call me?"

"Because he was a Jew. And he wanted—I want—a Jewish funeral service for him."

"So now you want my help! Take advantage." She couldn't control herself and words flew out of her mouth. "What *chutzpah*. You know what that means, don't you?" she said sarcastically. "So now you want an organized religion—you want me to provide the service, when he never supported us?"

"You are the only rabbi there."

"Only because Jews support me. They belong to the Center." She regretted arguing with the bereaved son, but her passion to protect her people overlook her impulse to console.

"I'll pay you. Don't worry about that. Whatever your fee."

"Please. Don't insult me. It's not about money."

"What, then?"

"My fee is membership in the Center."

"That was his decision, not mine."

"So, what synagogue do you belong to?"

"I believe like my father."

Sing, don't scream, she thought. She calmed a little.

"Look, whether he belonged or not is besides the point. He was a Jew. And so am I. And I am asking that you preside at a service for him."

"You should have thought about this before. Maybe if people like you joined . . . "

"You're right. OK? So what do you expect me to do, rabbi?"

"You should have thought about this before you needed me."

"But you are a rabbi. This is what you're supposed to do."

"I am supposed to care for the Jewish people. It's not fair that you call on us when you need us but you don't affiliate with us when we need you."

"Look," he said. "You're a rabbi. You have a duty. To all Jews. Especially at the time of death."

"I have a duty to Jews, all Jews, when they are alive, who

support the Jewish people, not to ones who die and turned their back on us."

"He never did anything against Jews. He was proud to be a Jew."

"That didn't do me—the Jewish Center—any good. With Jews like him there wouldn't be any synagogues at all."

And so the conversation looped and circled. Finally Ali ended it.

Until the next day when a reporter from the Associated Press wanted a quote from her, to defend herself.

And the following day calls from local TV stations, CNN, newspapers domestic and foreign. Magazines. Vile, vicious, cruel callers screaming, whispering, threatening: Woman. Socialist. Lesbian. Jew.

Until she stopped answering the phone.

But she had to explain herself first at a special meeting of the TJC, then to the Buffalo County Clergy Association. The same at both—a divided group; the same questions, the same support, the same accusations and disappointments. Her failure, ultimately, the inability to bring the group together. *Tikkun olam,* repairing the world, she learned at the cantorial school and she took it to heart, her mission through song and music. She couldn't repair her reputation, the Jewish Center, Christian-Jewish bonds.

Ali hummed a *niggun,* a wordless melody, as she searched for herself.

"How vast are your works, Adonai. Your designs are exceedingly profound," she sang to the text of Psalm 92.

So profound she didn't understand.

Then *Hine Ma Tov:* "How good and pleasant/When brothers

and sisters dwell in harmony." She sang at the service, the congregants, too, a hymn, a melody they all knew but the room was emptier than usual.

This could never be. Not for her. Here. She explained as she tendered her resignation from the pulpit. Not now. Someday.

Maybe.

LOVE THE ONE
YOU'RE WITH

*W*HEN MARCUS AND THEA DECIDED TO MARRY, they, like many couples, imagined their ideal future and, sure that their love was true, exchanged wedding vows at the West Side Community Christian Congregation, even though neither of them thought of themselves as religious. They wanted to honor their families' traditions. They pledged to be each other's life-long companions, take pleasure in each other's accomplishments and, remain together through whatever hardships that would befall them, and stay faithful to one another. In private they pledged to have a loving family, with two children—a girl and a boy—, although if both were the same sex, they had no preference which.

Approaching seven years of married life, the Wheelers took stock of their marriage. They made an inventory of their lives: their work was going well, they had good friends and they would choose each other as spouses again without hesitation. Life was good, but not perfect. The great sadness was that all four of their parents had died in the intervening years. Because of this they felt their lack of family more keenly—they were childless. When they finally acknowledged that there might be a physiological problem, they went to a fertility clinic. There they established a schedule for their sex lives—what time, how and how often, and under what conditions they were to have intercourse. What started as a romp, with quips such as, 'With medicine like this, who wouldn't want to be sick?' and cute pictures drawn on the calendar taped on the wall above the bed headrest, in six months became work, a tedious chore. Sex was no longer pleasurable and spiritual. Instead of being a shared joy, having sex was a duty, a regulated one at that. Thea's enthusiasm was stoked with a rekindled love for Marcus and the thought of what sex might bring, but Marcus's interest, to his great astonishment, waned. He found the regimentation distasteful. Sex became one more area of Marcus's life where he was measured by performance on demand. He was no longer sure whether Thea desired him or whether he was merely a means for her to another end. He was jealous of a child that didn't yet exist.

As a result of the burden Marcus felt, Thea's eagerness for sex also faded. She continued the program because she badly wanted her own family. But she also felt like a double failure—no longer attractive to Marcus and being unable to conceive. It turned out, though, that further tests revealed that it wasn't Thea who was the problem (a word they tried to avoid to describe their condition but couldn't) but Marcus. On the advice of the fertility specialist, Marcus switched from briefs to boxer shorts, stopped using the stationary bicycle at the gym and the hot tub after his workout; he gave up smoking marijuana, began taking vitamin supplements and drank ginseng tea while abstaining from coffee. He also visited an acupuncturist who claimed to have great success in curing male infertility. On the acupuncturist's wall were children's crayon drawings. Twice a week for six months, Marcus, with thin needles sticking from various parts of his body, stared at the pictures. When he told Thea that he wasn't going to see the acupuncturist any longer, she thought his complaint would be about being pricked with needles. Instead, he detested the silly drawings she displayed and Dr. Jenny's cloying attitude, treating him as though he were the child they were trying to create.

There were other options, Thea said. Marcus didn't care any longer. He could no longer imagine a life with a child.

"I know we wanted kids," Marcus said to his wife, his eyes wide open staring at the ceiling. "But the more we've tried the worse things have become."

"Between us, you mean?" Thea said, turning on her side to face him.

"I'm done with it. No kids. That's it."

Thea had thought about using donor sperm, but she would never suggest this to Marcus.

"I don't want to give up."

Marcus didn't respond.

Thea understood Marcus's silence. She had become good at interpreting that. Marcus put out the reading light on his side of the bed and fell asleep on his back; Thea put in earphones to listen to her playlist. She was nearly asleep when the Aretha Franklin cut came up on shuffle. She had always liked the song and knew it well. Now she heard it in a different way. "If you are confused/ And you don't remember who you're talkin' to . . ." When the song was over, she shut off her iPod and looked at Marcus who was sprawled on his back. She sang the refrain of the song to herself several times—'love the one you're with.' She didn't believe in signs, but she took the injunction to heart. Marcus was here with her and she did love him.

Before turning off her light on her side of the bed, she reached over to touch her husband's leg. She rested it there for a moment, then stroked his shoulder and breathed in deeply the salty smell of his skin. He mumbled something she couldn't understand and turned on his side facing the wall, and his breathing became deeper as he fell away from her.

*I*t took Thea several months before she had the courage to tell Marcus what she had been doing. She wanted this to come out right. If she presented it wrong, not only might this end the chances of having children, it could also mean the end of her marriage.

Her fears were unfounded. Rather than pushing him further away, Thea's revealing that she had been investigating adoption came as a relief to Marcus. No longer having to subject themselves to further tests and laboratories, they felt as though their marriage had been given back to them. They would have a child after all.

What they hadn't anticipated was that there would be more interviews, more explanations, more questionnaires, more scrutiny and more humiliation. Rather than feeling welcomed as new parents, they felt as though they needed to bare their inner selves—strangers with probing questions now pried into their lives. They had exchanged physicians for social workers. There were background checks, psychological tests and other procedures they found exhausting. And when they were finished, they were put on a waiting list years long and all that without a guarantee that there would be a child at the end.

A friend asked if they had considered international adoption, something they had thought about initially but had dismissed as each day they expected the adoption procedure to be completed. But now facing an indefinite delay, the question came as an epiphany. They wondered why they hadn't pursued that course sooner. So they began researching the possibility of adopting overseas. Marcus and Thea considered every country from which Americans regularly adopted and finally settled on Haiti, one close enough that they could visit regularly until the adoption became final.

Every spare minute was spent on the Internet researching. The numbers were staggering: 380,000 registered orphans, many left by families too poor to raise the children themselves. The Wheelers couldn't understand why, with such obvious and pressing need, it took up to three years to complete an adoption. So when they found Suffer the Children, an independent Christian agency in Virginia that sponsored La Chance Orphelinat Secondes, near Etang Saumatre, an orphanage caring for more than 100 children, that promised an expeditious process and had several testimonials from families that had adopted through them on their website, it became their choice. They contacted Suffer the Children and received an immediate and encouraging reply, via email, from Rev. Noreen Quimby, the founder and director. After filling out an online questionnaire, they received a telephone call from the founding pastor and director of the agency, who assured them that their application would be quickly processed and that would have a child in less than a year. "Of course, when dealing with a country like Haiti, there is always the unpredictable. But we have had much success there. Jesus wants these children to have a loving home."

The Wheelers sent a small processing fee to the agency, a sum considerably less than what other agencies had required. Rev. Quimby phoned again, this time to thank them for their "contribution to help save the children" and told them that the orphanage itself would shortly contact them.

Marcus and Thea were surprised when less than two weeks later, they received an email from Marie Auguste, the director of La Chance Orphelinat Secondes, with an attachment, a photo of Ghislaine, a neatly dressed two-year-old seated in front of a white-washed building with a corrugated blue metal roof, her braided hair fixed with pink and green wooden beads. She smiled prettily at the camera.

"What do you think?" Noreen Quimby asked. "Isn't she adorable?"

They agreed with her, absolutely. Thea bought a picture frame and placed the photo in it.

"Do you really think that is such a good idea?" Marcus asked, knowing what Thea's answer would be. "Maybe we should wait until this is final, when she's really ours. So many things can go wrong."

"Not this time. It won't. I know it."

Rev. Quimby called every few weeks. On one occasion she told them that they were expected to visit the orphanage at least once before the adoption could be finalized, so they could meet

Ghislaine in person. Everyone needed to make sure this was the right thing to do.

Thea couldn't contain her enthusiasm. But Marcus became skeptical when Rev. Quimby said that she would arrange for the air tickets and they should pay her directly. She then asked for additional money for the adoption. The amount now neared $10,000, still nearly the same that other agencies were requiring for international adoptions, but nearly twice as much as they had been led to believe what would be required.

Marcus knew that Thea would dismiss any doubts that he raised. And if he persisted, Thea's heart would take her to Haiti and away from him. When he did research on international adoption procedures, he saw that while Suffer the Children's approach was unorthodox, in some respects it wasn't unique. The need for homes for children was so great and the resources so scant that Marcus concluded that it was unreasonable to expect that things would be run as they were in the States. He wanted transparency and accountability from the agency, but that seemed impossible. However, as far as Marcus could tell everything that Suffer the Child did was legal, even as it shaved the edges. Having satisfied himself, Marcus put aside his own misgivings and, as each day passed, grew more loving towards Thea, as together they wrote letters to Ghislaine, and whenever they received a reply from the orphanage, which came with some regularity, their spirits were lifted together to heights they hadn't experienced since the days they first fell in love with one another. With each phone call from Rev. Quimby and letters from Haiti, they became more eager to see their daughter, to hold her, to bring her home. They talked about how they would raise her, bought parenting books,

discussed what nicknames they would give her and began scour-
ing the classifieds for a larger apartment, in a neighborhood with
better schools.

The FBI fingerprinted Thea and Marcus; a background check
was run on them. They passed psychological and physical exams.
Rev. Quimby offered assurances that all this was routine and, in
fact, everything was going very well. She remembered them in
all her prayers and she was certain that she was doing all that she
could to move the process along quickly. She had connections,
she said.

"You know what I mean."

Although the Wheelers knew that a home visit by a social
worker to assess their suitability as parents was a legal requirement, they resented the presumption that someone—anyone but
particularly a stranger—could make a judgment in a few hours
talk with them that would not only determine their future but
also that of a orphaned child, or that they needed to be judged
by anyone. Their suitability to become parents had never been
raised by the fertility clinics, why now by an adoption agency?
Knowing that they had no choice, that there would be no child
for them without the interrogation, they agreed. They rehearsed
what they would say, cleaned their apartment to new levels of
anti-sepsis, re-doubled the amount of reading they did about
raising children, adopted children, children adopted from Third
World countries, and about Haiti itself, testing one another on
the geography of western Hispaniola, finding the location of the
orphanage on a map that they hung above the television set in
the living room, and learning the difference between Creole and
French pronunciation. They needed to be expert parents in every

way, they thought, which, in their minds was ridiculous, if not insulting, but a necessary precaution they were willing to indulge, for the cost of failure was too great, one that they couldn't bear.

Another email from Suffer the Children said that a "Dr. Bien-Aime has gone over there to see Ghislaine and you have a healthy, on-target child and you should take great assurance in that," which they did. When the formal report didn't arrive within a month, the Wheelers were promised that it was on its way. "This is Haiti and you know how things are there. But we can thank Jesus," she tacked on, as she did when she ended most conversations.

The home inspection was anti-climactic—a brief and cordial visit by a plain woman, one who looked like she had just graduated from a college that frowned upon make-up or a dress that wouldn't be found left-over even in a Goodwill store. She politely refused a cup of coffee but did cheerfully accept a Cola. She asked some questions, took notes and walked from room to room in bright curiosity, without a hint of condescension.

Relieved that they had worked themselves into a state of anxiety for no reason, Thea could hardly contain her enthusiasm a week later when they received a call from Rev. Quimby telling them that their dossier had been sent to an official department in Haiti, where it would be reviewed. This was usually the point in which the process became "thick with many hands," she said. But, hadn't everything gone right until now? The pastor told them that she had a dream about Marcus and Thea, with Ghislaine, in a beautiful blue house and they were all very happy.

"Do you have a dog?" she asked unexpectedly.

"No."

She saw one in the vision, but that didn't matter. She trusted her dreams.

As if by miracle, two months later they were approved. Ghislaine had been granted a passport. The schedule had been moved up. Although the usual procedure was to make a preliminary visit to the orphanage before taking the child home to the States, Suffer the Children was going to dispense with this step.

"Jesus visited me and told me that you were the parents, you were the ones. What should I do, Jesus, I asked and He said that you were beautiful people and I should follow my heart." Their first visit to Haiti would be the only one necessary for the adoption. "I hope that the two of you are able to go by the end of next month," the pastor said.

"Are you kidding?" Thea shouted into her phone, her face turning hot with excitement. The news was too good to be true. "I' m ready to go tomorrow."

"Well," Rev. Quimby said in her supportive but authoritative tone, "there still is paper work to be completed."

And the remaining $10,000, she added, dropping this casually, as though it were no more significant than a change of email address, although this was the first that Thea had heard that more money was due. This now brought the total to $30,000.

"Yes, of course, we'll get it to you right away," Thea said, certain that she must have been wrong, that Rev. Quimby had told them before, that she simply wasn't remembering correctly. While concerned about the additional money, Thea knew that amount was within the bounds of costs for foreign adoptions. Before they had found Suffer the Children, it was what they were willing to pay. They had the money.

Anticipating Marcus's skepticism and growing dislike and distrust of the pastor, Thea could only say, "I know . . . I know what you are thinking, Marcus. But please, don't make me say . . ."—that the Rev. Quimby was smarmy, that she was a fraud, that the program was a scam, that they were throwing good money after bad, that they were chasing their losses, that the adoption may be illegal . . . all that may be true, but what if it weren't? There was Ghislaine, the girl with the broad smile, the plaits and the pink and green beads, the one whose photo they had framed and sat on the dresser in the bedroom. It was for her that they had to put aside their misgivings and that, having received the documents needed for Ghislaine to leave Haiti, were ready to go to the island to bring the child— their child—home.

"You go, Marcus," Thea said when the pastor called to tell them the date was set for them to pick up their child. "I'll stay home and get everything ready." She couldn't believe she was suggesting this and that she was going to wait even longer to touch her and smell her. "I really don't think I could stand to see her in an orphanage. I don't want to have that image of her in my head." She also thought that Marcus's holding Ghislaine, needing to care for her on his own, was the best way for him to overcome his reservations. Besides, she admitted to him with a hint of shame, she was frightened of going to such a poor and dangerous country.

$\mathcal{N}$ow that he arrived, Marcus was glad that Thea wasn't with him. They had looked at photographs, watched documentaries and YouTube videos about Haiti and knew the statistics about Haitian poverty, but Marcus was unprepared for what he saw the moment he stepped into the tropical sun at Toussaint Louverture International Airport, walked across the shimmering tarmac in the mid-afternoon to the terminal and then outside and into a taxi—miles of half-completed buildings with rebar pointing at the clear sky like gnarled, iron fingers, debris and rocks where there had once been pavement, goats and dogs rooting through garbage, children half-dressed and shoeless, beggars at each road stop, and the sweet smell of cooking food mixed with that of rancid oil and charcoal. His head reeled from it all, the heat and the aromas and the sights.

When the taxi tipped forward and titled on its side, Marcus was hurtled from the backseat to the front of the car. The air was filled with smoke and dust.

"My God. Earthquake," the driver said in English, then rattled off a string of sentences that Marcus couldn't understand.

The two of them pushed against the door on the passenger's side, squeezed out, then with great effort pushed the car back onto its four wheels. Around them buildings had collapsed, corrugated roofs peeled off, the road completely gone. Trees were uprooted.

"I have to get you back to the airport," the driver said. "You have to go home. I have to go to my family. Look. Look. This is bad. This is very, very bad."

"How much further is it to Etang Saumatre?" Marcus wanted to know. "How long to the orphanage?"

"You can't go there. You have to go home. This is no good. No good. This is no good here. Just look!"

The driver got back into the car and tried to start the engine. "No good."

After a few more turns of the key, the engine kicked over.

"Get in," he demanded.

The driver maneuvered the car around the rubble and began to turn back towards Port-au-Prince.

"Where are you going?" Marcus shouted.

"You have to be safe. I can get you back to the airport."

Marcus, without a thought, shouted, "I'm not going back. Take me to the orphanage. I have to get my daughter."

"That's not going to be possible."

Marcus took out his money from a pouch that hung around his neck and thrust a fist-full of bills into the driver's hand. The driver looked at the money and turned the car around again.

The car radio wasn't working, but as they traveled they asked people along the road what had happened. The capital city was cut off but they heard that it had been destroyed. Even the president's palace had collapsed. Haiti was isolated from the rest of the world.

Still they continued eastward. Roads were nearly impassable, as they were strewn with rocks and blocked by downed lines and trees. The driver knew his way through valleys and across hills now shrouded in night darkness. They left the trunk road and followed what seemed to Marcus to be no more than cow paths and walk lanes. The only light was from the car's headlights and that of a lantern from a lone pedestrian.

Fatigued from the long ride, where he had napped intermittently throughout the night, his back and head aching from the jouncing, Marcus arrived at La Chance Orphelinat Secondes. It had taken them all night to go twenty miles. When Marcus stepped out of the car, his strength returned, even as he was overwhelmed by what he saw and he had not eaten in nearly a day.

The green metal signboard for La Chance Orphelinat Secondes, about ten meters by six, was thrust into the ground upside down as though thrown like a spear; the iron fence surrounding the compound lay twisted on its side, and the concrete dormitory was in rubble. The front wall of another house was gone, exposing the inside like that of a cut-away dollhouse, the furniture undisturbed. A boulder that had tumbled from the mountainside left a swath of destruction on the hillside behind the compound and stopped just short of the pink office building that stood unscathed. Children and adults sat, bandages over wounds, limbs twisted in impossible directions; cries and moans filled the air.

On the lawn were blankets and sheets covering more than a dozen bodies, many of them small. Marcus looked at each girl, most covered with dust and blood, comparing them to the photo in his hand, and he called her name out loud. He asked several if they were Ghislaine, but no one answered him. The only sounds were cries and moans and that of shovels hitting stone.

A woman approached Marcus and looked at the photo he showed her.

"Ghislaine," he said.

"Yes, I know," the woman said, and pointed him to bodies covered with sheets that were laid out on the lawn near the flagpole that still stood. Johanne pulled back the shroud and Marcus looked briefly at the girl, recognizing her only from the beads in her braids, the same ones that she wore in photo that was folded in his pocket. He covered her again with the thin blanket and his knees buckled. When he recovered his strength, he lifted her from the grass and placed her in a shallow grave by the boulder, then another child on top of her and took a shovel so he would cover her with the thin soil himself.

Later in the day, when his mind cleared, he realized that Thea hadn't heard from him since he had gone through customs the day before, when he called to say that he was fine and laughed about wearing shirtsleeves while she was bundled up trying to stay warm in the winter weather. She would be frantic watching the news on TV—where was he, was he safe, what about Ghislaine, were they together, when would bring her home?—and worry coursed through him. But there was no way to reach her. Whatever passable roads there had been were blocked and gone; there were no working telephones; flights in and out of Haiti were canceled; entire areas of the country were cordoned off; everything he saw, everything he heard led to the same conclusion: Haiti had succumbed to the earth's sharp fury. He looked for the taxi; it was gone with his luggage and the supplies and gifts he had brought for Ghislaine and the orphanage.

Despite the isolation or perhaps because of it, Marcus felt redoubled in his efforts to help. He only stopped digging and hauling, wiping, binding and holding when he couldn't move any longer, when he retched on his empty stomach.

In the dark, Marcus was shaken awake.

"Monsieur."

Standing above him was a young woman holding a child whose head rested on her shoulder.

"I am Johanne. I am an assistant nurse," she said. "I have a new Ghislaine for you."

As his eyes adjusted to the dark, he saw that a few feet away another woman stared at him. Her torn dress exposed her right shoulder and her legs were white with the dust of concrete.

"Your Ghislaine has been taken by God, but he has given you another," she said. "I have found Ghislaine's file under the rubble. Everything you need is here. This girl, she needs a home, too."

When Marcus stood, the woman gave the girl to him. Before he could think, he took her and held her against his chest.

The girl woke momentarily, then adjusted her body, and settled back into sleep. He could feel her breath on his neck.

Marcus was as mute as the nearby woman. The girl, who had been washed and cleaned, snuffled.

"How can I take her?"

"How can you not?"

"She's not my daughter."

"Take her, please."

"I can't leave. I want to stay . . ." Marcus was nearly hysterical in his protestation.

"You can save one life," Johanne insisted. "This one, you can take care of it forever. If you stay, we have to care for you, too."

Johanne thrust Ghislaine's folder under Marcus's arm. He took it into his hand.

"There's a boat at the lake. It can take you to the Dominican Republic. If you get there before morning, it would be best. The driver knows where to drop you on the other side." She then asked, "Do you have money?"

Marcus felt for the purse he had hung around his neck and under his shirt. It was still there.

"You need some for the boat and maybe to give to the guards on the other side." She didn't ask for herself or the orphanage. He felt relieved.

In the D.R. he could call Thea. But if he stayed at the orphanage or even attempted to get back to Port-au-Prince, there was no way of knowing how long it would take before he could talk to her and assure her of his safety.

"I can get out of Haiti tonight?"

"Yes."

"Then take me," he said, holding out the child out for Johanne to take.

She pushed the girl back against Marcus.

"You have to take her. You see what is here. If she stays, there is no food, there is no medicine. We have nothing. What will happen to her? You tell *me.*"

"I can't do that. I can't take her. She's not mine."

"We have too many suffering children. This is one that you can help. God wants you to take her."

Hearing that, Marcus' unease was stirred again. But when he put his hand on the back of the child's head to reposition her on his shoulder, she nuzzled against him, wrapped her arms around his neck and whimpered from some pain which he could only begin to imagine. She woke and began to squirm. The folder fell to the ground.

"Here," Johanne said, reaching down and picked up the fallen papers. "Are you going to take it?" She put the thick file in front of him. "Are you going to go to America with your Ghislaine? Isn't that why you came?"

Johanne took Marcus by the elbow. He resented being manipulated by her, but he let her lead him to a grove of trees. The child was asleep again.

"He will take you to the lake," she said to Marcus. Johanne spoke rapidly in Creole to the man who took the folder from him. Marcus felt a nudge on his back. He turned around and the woman who had been standing nearby looked into his eyes and in a soft voice speaking Creole handed him a small cloth bag.

"For the child," Johanne said, and the woman stood still as she and Marcus continued across the broad opening towards the lake. When Marcus looked back, the woman was gone.

Marcus climbed into the skiff and placed the child down on the plank of the open boat and he sat beside her. She leaned against him as the boat putted in the darkness, the only sound that of the engine and the water slapping against its bow. He felt nauseated by the fumes and splashed water on his face. Marcus thought about what he would say to Thea when he placed the call to her in the next few hours.

"We have our child," he said to himself, rehearsing the conversation, convincing himself that the child was really with him, that the two of them would be home soon, that he and Thea would come into her room at night to look at her, having fulfilled their dream of having a family. He had no idea what he—they—would tell Ghislaine, as he knew that one day she would ask about her life in Haiti.

Marcus fingered Ghislaine's pouch that was on the seat beside him. He picked it up and dangled it over the side of the boat. Instead of dropping it into the water, he returned it to his lap. He and Thea would open it together. He then put his hands into the lake to quench his thirst and scooped a handful of water in his palm. He choked on the salt water and vomited.

The boat drifted towards the shingle beach where border guards, waiting for the day to begin, dozed in the dark. As the sky lightened Marcus marveled at the deep blue of the saline water. In the distance were pink flamingoes and as the boat neared the shore a crocodile plunged into the water and disappeared from view.

LEMON

"*T*HIS ISN'T JUST YOUR DECISION TO MAKE, WAL-ter," Roseline said. The church president sat with her hands fold-ed on her lap, her youthful-looking face shining under a halo of tight white curls of hair. As always, she was impeccably dressed. "It affects us all." Roseline leaned forward, selected an almond biscotti from the candy dish on the coffee table and nodded as Walter poured her a steaming cup of tea. The cookie snapped as she bit into it. Roseline brushed the crumbs into a napkin. "The congregation supported you on everything you've done. Espe-cially Emmet and me."

"Yes, that's more than true," Walter Braithwaite said with gen-uine appreciation. "I can't have asked anything more than what the two of you have done for me and my family." Walter recalled the many times in which Roseline and her late husband defended him, particularly during the first few years of his tenure, when members wanted to fire him over his—lack of experience, poor judgment, emotionalism, not spending enough time with the

40

frail and elderly, spending too much time on community affairs, his uninspired sermons, focusing too much time on the church's youth and, because he did not yet have children himself, his inability to understand family life, all charges containing a kernel of truth.

When Walter was installed at the United Church of Christ of Fairview a dozen years ago, the church was content in its quietism. It was a solid congregation of professionals who enjoyed tempered gospel singing, a little exuberance and Sunday socializing. Living an upright life and avoiding scandal was enough for them. But Walter, fresh out of seminary, challenged them. More than rectitude, he wanted justice. His agreement with the board of elders when they appointed him was that while he would consult with them before he brought new programs and procedures to the church, they needed to give him room to innovate. Jesus challenged the powers of his time, the young Rev. Braithwaite said, and today's Christians needed to do the same. "If you don't like what I do, you can dismiss me. But give me a chance. We have to change to stay relevant." He marshaled the theories he had learned in school but it wasn't his ideas that won them over but his sincerity. In his inaugural sermon, he talked about the dual role of the church and his place in it: to comfort the afflicted and to afflict the comfortable; prick deep enough to wound and offer salve to heal. He spoke to the congregants, about them, for them, although, to his dismay, most heard the first part of the message as being directed at others, while taking too seriously the second part as applying to themselves.

Walter held himself to the standard he set for others, ceaselessly examining his own conscience and motives. But some couldn't abide by the changes. For the first few years it wasn't at all certain that he would stay, but he succeeded in winning enough support that gradually pride replaced self-satisfaction in the congregation, in no small measure because of Roseline and Emmet's guidance. They served as the Braithwaite's tutors. The turn towards activism was reflected in a dentist who gave up his practice to represent the district in Congress; Walter's chairmanship of the county Human Rights Commission; and the church's successful initiation of an ecumenical soup kitchen. Under Walter's direction, the church bought a housing complex that was converted into an owner's cooperative. UCCF adopted a sister church in Ghana and the church guaranteed the first year of the college tuition for the valedictorian of the local high school there.

"You know we've never had a minister as beloved as you. And we still admire you, Walter. More than ever." Roseline spoke not as a church official but as a friend.

"I know that and appreciate it," Walter said sincerely. "I always have. It means a great deal to me."

The vocal and unstinting support from Roseline and Emmet had helped him get through the roughest parts: when Gwen started a group for abused women and some parishioners confided in her that they themselves were victims; when Walter opened church doors first to Alcoholics Anonymous, then embraced a gay man who joined the church. A leading elder and his wife left the church over this, saying that they were afraid of being infected with AIDS by touching a door knob or eating off a church plate.

Roseline had called to see him and suggested they meet in the house, not his office.

"And it's because I love you that I need to tell you. Not this.

It's more than you that's involved. The entire congregation is in this together."

The entire church, Walter thought. It always seemed to come down to that. He understood that well enough and he accepted the burden—never being an individual, always the ever-vigilant role model who was his church's face to the world. They were his flock, he was their surrogate, and so how he looked and what he did mattered to everyone. This careful calibration of his image and personality came with the career that he had chosen.

There were thoughts that he couldn't express, doubts that crept around the edges of his theology. He could never admit that he had reservations about his childhood friend—"the finest person I have ever known"—going to hell because of his suicide or that when he attended a commitment ceremony for his lesbian cousin, he wished that it was he that had been the officiant.

He and Roseline sat in the living room, the afternoon sun streaming through the white curtained window, but whose house was this? The congregants called it his house, Walter's, their minister, but he didn't own it. He wasn't like other homeowners. He didn't hold the mortgage or pay property taxes. Neither did he pay rent. Part of the salary they paid him ("we know that it is too little"; "you deserve more and we'll give it to you when we can afford it") came in the form of the parsonage, a Cape Cod house with dormers in a suburban middle-class neighborhood, repairs, maintenance and lawn care included, all under the supervision of a church committee that had the final word before any changes could be made. And there was nothing he could do about the person (there was always one) who surreptitiously examined the tidiness and cleanliness of the household whenever he visited.

He and Gwen felt as if they were guests in the house. But he could never say that, even to the parishioners who he and Gwen had befriended. They talked about buying their own home, but they couldn't afford it, particularly with Gwen staying home to take care of the children.

He wished that Roseline would leave. Gwen would be home soon with Malcolm from his nursery school and Walter didn't want to have this conversation with their son present.

"From the beginning, we've done what we can. Tell me what else I can do to help."

"There isn't anything. You've done more than anyone could have asked. But this is my decision," he said without conviction.

"What about Gwen?"

"Mine and Gwen's."

"She goes along with this?" Roseline asked.

"Roseline," he said, "do you think that I would decide this without her?" Walter shook his head. Roseline's looked directly into his eyes.

"This is the most difficult decision of my life."

"Then don't do it. We'll all chip in. You have taught us not to be like crabs in a barrel but like bees in a hive," Roseline said, quoting from Walter's favorite images of greed and cooperation.

Roseline and Emmet had always been major financial contributors to the church and from now on, Roseline said, she would turn over her Social Security checks directly to the Braithwaite's to help with whatever additional burdens they may bear.

𝒲alter's predecessors at UCCF had arrived married and with their children, so June's baptism had been an especially joyous occasion. A senior minister from the metropolitan area, Walter's mentor at the seminary, assisted with the baptism service. The social hall was freshly painted mint green and tables were decorated with red and white roses; members brought their best covered-dishes and a special cake was ordered from the area's premier bakery, a triple-layer chocolate covered confection with small plastic figures of June, Gwen and Walter perched on top.

June became the parish's child, spoiled by everyone, adored and pampered. She thrived in the light of attention. One advantage of being a minister, Walter discovered, was that he had time to be a father and husband in new ways. Aside from Sundays and the many nighttime meetings, Walter controlled his own schedule. This allowed Gwen to develop a social work practice while Walter brought June to the bus stop in the morning, arranged doctor's visits, shopped for food, did laundry, vacuumed, washed dishes and picked up his daughter after school. Initially seen as scandalous and even shameful, it took several years for the Braithwaites' egalitarian marriage to be accepted; it was when Gwen, at Roseline's suggestion, took on the position as head of the women's brigade that she won the women over. And when Emmet pointed out to the board of elders that Walter's domesticity didn't detract from his pastoral duties, male parishioners first forgave, then understood and finally legitimated his behavior.

The Braithwaite marriage became the measure of marital relationships in the church and was even more celebrated when they announced that they would adopt their second child.

"There are so many children in need," Walter sermonized. "God provides for all, but He requires us to be His servants. Jesus said, 'I wish everyone were like little children, for the Kingdom of God belongs to such as these.'

"We must provide for each. And we each must do what we can. The little angels that have descended in our midst sometimes make a hard landing. These heavenly wayfarers must also be clothed and fed."

Taking in a child wasn't unusual for families in the church. But generally they were a niece or nephew; a few were raising their grandchildren. No one adopted a stranger's child.

Walter broached the idea of adoption to Gwen.

"We already have an angel," she said defensively. "We don't know what we will get when we adopt."

She thought about foster children who often bring with them wounds and scars beyond repair.

"You *never* know what you'll get," he responded. "God gave us a gift the first time, but we can't know what another child will be like. You do want another child, don't you?"

"I think about it every once in a while," she said. "It would be hard, but yes, I do."

Walter laughed. "Well, this is the express train. We can have a kid without the nine stops in between. No morning sickness, no stretch marks."

Gwen was unconvinced. Over the next few years, Walter quietly persisted. Her desire for an larger family grew the more Walter spoke about the virtues of an additional child, how their love for each other would expand, how his heart broke thinking about unloved children and how much they, all three, had to give to the world. And he was right, she thought—there was something selfish about bearing a child when one was already waiting to be loved.

When Gwen told Walter that she was ready to adopt, he waited until the idea had firmly settled before mentioning his next idea.

"The greatest need is for older children to find homes," he said.

Again, he was right. Gwen couldn't impeach Walter's heart but something else was at stake. Once more thoughts of foster children entered her mind.

"What about June?" she asked.

"What about her?"

"It's one thing to have an infant. She'll get used to that. She'll be jealous, but she'll get used to it and she'll be the loving big sister."

"June will, I know," Walter agreed.

"But it's different if you bring in an older child." She hesitated. She wanted to say this right, but she couldn't express her real fear. "I don't think it's a good idea. We have to think about June. I'm worried about her. What this will mean to her. Why not become foster parents, let's see what it's like?"

"That's like living together without being married," he said, knowing this was something they both disapproved of. Walter hugged her. He said, "It will mean that she'll have a brother who will love her, just like we do."

She felt small and uneasy in his arms. Gwen began to quiver and couldn't explain to Walter why her eyes welled with tears.

Gwen confided in Roseline her concerns about adopting an older child.

"Where there is great love there are always miracles," Roseline recited Willa Cather's aphorism to Gwen. "Emmet and I will be

glad to be the godparents. It is a big step, but Walter has challenged us to take big steps before and he was right. He has afflicted the comfortable and we've been made better for it. Just as
we have set up a trust for June, we'll set one up for this child, too."

It wasn't the money, Gwen said. But she couldn't articulate
what was bothering her. She felt shamed by her reservations, less
a Christian than she ought to be, not an acceptable feeling for a
minister's wife. She never revealed her qualms again.

Walter and Gwen looked through The Heart Gallery photos
provided by the Office of Foster Care and Adoption Services,
each child smiling as if this were their school yearbook picture.
The Braithwaite's sat with the pictures and read and re-read each
of the children's stories until they selected a ten year-old boy, the
one with buck teeth and glasses, the sun glinting off his forehead
and his hands clasped as though in prayer. By the time they were
approved, a quick process because they were such a desirable family, Gwen was as committed to her Malcolm as was Walter.

For months June happily chattered about having a new brother,
but her enthusiasm wilted when she saw the photo of the child
they had selected.

"It's not a baby," she cried. "It's a boy!"

Gwen picked her up and sat her on her lap, and they talked.

"Of course, he's a boy. He's your big brother."

"I don't want him," she sobbed. "I want a baby to play with."

Walter and Gwen paid more attention to June than ever and
patiently told her the advantages of having an older brother; they
cajoled, they soothed and sang and dreamed and played and gave
her more of what she asked for until a flood of attention and
promises overcame June's resistance.

In anticipation of his arrival, Walter and Gwen, with June's help, painted the guest room, now known as 'Malcolm's room.' Arrangements were made at school and the church planned a gala, much like June's welcome five years earlier. They bought a boy's bicycle and, knowing that he enjoyed puzzles, put several in his room.

The Braithwaite's house was filled with balloons and other decorations chosen by June when Malcolm arrived and June was thrilled when she shared the spotlight with Malcolm at the welcoming party at the church. But her mood changed within a week. She became sour and sullen and was often cross with her new brother. She frequently refused to acknowledge Malcolm's presence and always sat between her parents at grace so she wouldn't have to hold his hand. She cried when Gwen directed her attention towards her brother. For the first time June had trouble with other children in school and was punished for pushing another child.

"I hate him," June blurted out, ignoring Malcolm, who was standing next to Gwen.

"You don't hate him," Gwen said.

"That's a terrible thing to say, June. He's your brother."

"No he's not. He's not my brother. I hate him. He is somebody else's brother. Bring him back."

"Malcolm, please go to your room. I'll be there in a minute. Do your homework," Walter said. "I'll be right in to help you study."

Malcolm stifled his cry and walked away, leaving the door ajar. He picked up his math book and said half-aloud, "I don't need any help."

"He's horrible."

"We can't return him," Gwen said. June began to sob.

"Yes, you can. You took him here. You can take him back. He has lots of brothers and sisters where he came from."

Walter shot back, "No we can't. We can't just return him. We didn't buy Malcolm. He's not a toy."

Gwen took his hand to calm him down.

"You're not a baby any longer, June. Just accept it. He's your brother. That's it."

"No he isn't."

"Don't sass me, young lady."

"It's OK, Walter." Gwen tried to soothe her husband and daughter.

There was no consoling June that night, even as Walter and Gwen took her into their bed. Malcolm fidgeted in his own bed.

But June was right. They could return Malcolm. Before bringing him home, they learned that the adoption wouldn't be finalized for a year. During that period, the state could take the child away and return him to foster care. The Braithwaite's dismissed this proviso as debasing, an insult to their soon-to-be expanded family.

"There's no lemon law for children," Walter said. "My God, he's not a thing but a person." Half-jokingly he and Gwen planned on visiting their families in Barbados and remaining there in exile, if it came to that. This was their family and they weren't going to let a court or anyone take their child away. June would come around.

Malcolm, it turned out, was quiet and polite and deeply wary. Slowly he allowed June to touch him but winced when Walter put his arm around him. When he was chastised, no matter how slight, he hung his head and apologized.

"I'm sorry, Ma'am," he said.

"Mom," Gwen corrected.

"Please don't send me away."

"*I* wanted to talk to you without Gwen here," Roseline said.

"You know how persuasive you can be, Walter, and how loyal she is to you. I didn't want to put her in the position of defending you. She would have to do that in front of me. She's such a good wife. I think I know her well enough . . ." Roseline stumbled. "She's talked to me and the other women of the brigade . . . she loves Malcolm as much as her own child. As June."

Walter's mind filled with retorts, with many explanations. He could be very convincing and knew that he would be able to make Roseline understand. But he said nothing. He couldn't betray Gwen or June. He would take the blame for the decision, take it alone, allowing him to be seen as the failure, the fraud.

"I know that she doesn't agree with you."

*I*t was the other way round; it was Walter who came to agree with Gwen. At first he dismissed his wife's concerns about what was happening to June as being overly solicitous. Her expectations were unrealistic, he said. Of course, June would have a hard time. They knew that. All children want to preserve their places. No child wants to share her parents' affections. But June didn't adjust and, in time, Walter, too, began to worry.

"Some jewelry of mine is missing," Gwen told him. "I can't find the ring you bought me last year."

"You must have misplaced it."

"I looked everywhere."

The ring remained missing.

Shortly afterwards Walter found that his wallet, which he kept on top of his armoire, had been opened and the two ten dollars bills he always kept in it were gone.

The next week June told Gwen that she saw Malcolm with the ring.

"He put it in his pocket," June said. "He was playing with it and then put it in his pocket. I saw him do it."

Malcolm denied knowing anything about the ring and volunteered to help Gwen look for it. She glared at him and Malcolm's mouth began to twitch.

"Is there something you want to tell me? Lying will only make it worse."

"No, Ma'am."

"You're not helping yourself, Malcolm."

He stood silently.

"I'll ask you again. Did you take my ring?"

Malcolm wiped his running nose with the back of his hand.

"June . . ." he began.

" . . . saw you," Gwen finished. "What did you do with it? If you tell me the truth, it will be much easier for you than living with a guilty conscience. God knows everything."

Walter searched Malcolm's room but didn't find the ring. His punishment was not being allowed to play with his friends after school for a month.

June's mood improved during Malcolm's punishment. She agreed to sit next to him at dinner and asked him to help her with her homework. But as soon as Malcolm was permitted to visit with his friends again, June's mood plunged deeper than ever. She complained about having a fever, a sore throat, an aching tummy, and didn't want to go to school. She pleaded to stay home. She wedged between her parents during grace. She ate little. Each night she cried when they finished reading her a story and sometime before Gwen and Walter turned off their lights for the night, she was standing at the foot of their bed holding her cotton blanket and sucking her thumb. It was clear to the Braithwaites that June's anxiety was related to Malcolm. But they thought that it had been long enough for her to adjust.

In the privacy of their bed, after June had been returned to her own bed, Gwen shared June's concerns with Walter in the dark. They lay side-by-side.

"He's only a boy, Gwen. I'll tell you something I've never confessed to anyone before. When I was his age, my friend Clarence and I were caught shoplifting. It was the candy store we used to go to all the time. I don't know why we did it. We had money to buy what we wanted. Thank God the owner never told our parents. He just scared the hell out of us by saying that the next time he would call the cops and get us locked up in the state pen."

"Did you ever steal from your parents?"

"No."

"So it's different."

"With love, we grow out of it. I wasn't always a man of the cloth, you know. We can give Malcolm that love."

Gwen turned towards Walter. She touched his cheek. "I am finding it hard to love him. Not the way a mother should. I know it's my fault . . ."

"No it's not."

"But I don't know about him, Walter. He's too quiet. Too polite. It's like he has locked up something inside himself that isn't good."

"We all have our own devils to wrestle with, Gwen."

"Something about him scares me."

"I think it's June you're scared for."

"Is that wrong?"

Walter thought that it was, until the next incident, when June told Gwen what she had seen. Malcolm was in his room but the door was open. He was in his underwear and turned to look at June when he noticed her there. He was scratching his "private thing" and asked her to come into his bedroom.

"But I didn't, Mommy. I ran away."

As soon as he did it, Walter regretted slapping Malcolm across the face, but he, too, was frustrated by Malcolm's passivity and his lack of candor. Fortunately, the bruise didn't swell and was barely visible on his dark skin. Malcolm wouldn't say anything, so his teacher wouldn't have to report an incident to Child Protective Services. And he and Gwen hoped that June, too, would remain quiet. They didn't want anyone else involved. There was enough shame as it was. The best thing to do was bring back Malcolm on their own and admit to their failure to provide him with a loving home. Perhaps another family would do better. Perhaps he would be different in a family that wasn't the center of a church's attention or in a family with a girl.

They had tried. At least this much was more than most were willing to do. This is what he said to Gwen and June. But he felt the blame as his own.

"*T*he decision has been made, Roseline," Walter said. "There's no more to be said." He rubbed the side of his mouth with his forefinger.

"I'm very disappointed in you, Walter." Roseline pursed her lips. He felt her eyes drilling him. "I wish Emmet were here to talk to you."

"I have done my praying, Roseline, I assure you."

Walter couldn't look at his guest. "This has been the most difficult decision of my life. But it's done."

"Do you know what this might do to Malcolm? To the church?"

Walter didn't want to hear more; he couldn't hear any more. He felt sick. And he didn't want to be angry with Roseline.

"I won't interfere in your marriage, so I won't talk to Gwen. Please reconsider what you are doing."

"I have another appointment. I have to go. Excuse me, please." He stood and helped Roseline to her feet.

When Roseline left, Walter put on a wool sweater to stop his chills. It didn't help. He hoped Gwen would be home soon.

SHILA

*T*HE FIRST TIME SHILA SAID SHE PREFERRED NOT
to was when her mother told her what she was planning to pre-
pare for lunch.

"But you like hotdogs," Rena said.

"I *used* to like them," Shila offered as an explanation.

"What's changed your mind?"

Shila shrugged her shoulders.

"You liked them just last week."

"They're disgusting," she said without emotion.

Shila often described things she didn't like as disgusting, but
hotdogs were one of her favorite foods.

"Why do you say that? Why are they disgusting?"

Shila stood with her head slightly drooped and her lanky hair
brushed against her hunched shoulders.

"They just are."

"You must give me a better reason than that, Shila," Rena said,
using a familiar refrain, as she always encouraged her daughter

to explain the choices she made. Rena believed that this would help shape her daughter into a good person. Needing to present good reasons and encouraging her to think for herself would, she maintained, create a person who wouldn't be bullied by crowds. Rationality and gentleness were the keys to raising a good child, Rena believed.

Rena knew that there was nothing she could do to make Shila happy, not after Shila's father's death from a painful illness at an early age. Shila knew him only from photos in an album. She couldn't remember his voice or his smell. Still, Rena could still raise a thoughtful and kind daughter.

"What is it, Shila?" she gently nudged her.

"I don't want to eat dogs," Shila finally said.

"Oh," her mother laughed, putting the package back in the refrigerator. "I get it. Shila," she said, "they aren't made from dogs, you know. They're just *called* hot dogs."

"It's not funny. You hurt my feelings. Don't laugh at me."

"You're right. I shouldn't laugh. I'm sorry." She sat on the sofa and pulled Shila next to her.

"If they aren't made from dogs, why are they called that?" Shila asked fretfully.

"I don't know," Rena said. "But they're not made from dogs. I promise."

"Still." Shila remained unmoved.

"What if we called them frankfurters, instead?" Rena offered. "Will you eat them, then?"

"I prefer not to."

And she didn't, ever again, eat hotdogs, although for a while she did eat pizza with mushrooms, peppers and sausage. Until twelve, when she realized that beef was cow, pork was pig—animals that had personalities, animals on TV shows she had watched to learn her ABC's.

"Do you want sausage on your pizza?" Rena asked one day.

Having recently learned what sausage was made from, Shila answered, "I prefer not to."

Soon Shila stopped eating steaks and burgers, foods she once adored. She said she could no longer eat anything that had a face or walked on four legs or had a mother. Since none of these qualities applied to poultry, she continued to eat chicken and turkey, until she watched a documentary in her eighth-grade class on factory farming that showed chickens being debeaked and tossed into shredding machines and explained how selective breeding leads to fractures and chronic pain in the birds. She saw turkeys crowded together in sheds; dead ones needed to be culled daily from the crush of birds. Her mother, too, was horrified when at Shila's suggestion the two of them watched the video together. Rena promised she would never again buy poultry processed at factory farms.

But Shila wanted more. It didn't matter how the birds were raised—eating chickens was something she preferred not to do. Animal factory farms were completely horrifying and unworthy of human beings, both she and her mother agreed, but eating something that once had a life, like hers, something that ran away when threatened, was cruel in and of itself. Eating flesh of any kind was something that Shila refused to do.

Several years after her decision to give up meat, when she took a class in philosophy, Shila also gave up on God. Her mother found out when she reminded Shila that it was time for the two of them to attend the service for the dead at the temple, a ritual they had engaged in annually on the anniversary of her father's death, but this year Shila said, "I prefer not to."

Rena didn't argue with her and suggested that, instead, they light candles in their home.

"I can't believe in a god that isn't good," Shila said.

"I don't know why God took your father, Shila," her mother said soothingly. "There are some things we can never understand."

"It isn't that," Shila said.

"What then?"

"Food," Shila said. "I've been thinking about that. I read a book in the library." She quoted from *The Devil's Dictionary:* "'Edible: Good to eat, and wholesome to digest, as a worm to a toad, a toad to a snake, a snake to a pig, a pig to a man, and a man to a worm.' People eat animals. But animals also eat animals. Cats eat mice. Big fish eat little fish. The world exists on predators and prey. If God was good, why did he make a world where one animal has to kill another in order to live? Since he could have made whatever he wanted, that must mean that he wants animals to suffer. That's cruel. So either God isn't good or maybe there isn't even a god. If God isn't good, I don't want to worship Him. And if God doesn't exist, then there's nothing to believe in."

"In memory of your father, then," Rena said. "Let's light them for him."

"I prefer not to," she said.

That night, before dinner, without a prayer, her mother lit

a candle while Shila sat in her room. She never went to temple again.

Shila's mother was proud of her daughter's thoughtfulness and envied her calmness. It was as though Shila was reaching deep inside herself to something steady and sure. She found Shila's solid assuredness combined with her compassion reassuring in a world that was indifferent to serious things.

Her pride swelled when Shila set aside a portion of her wages from her job in a clothing store after school and donated it to a charity—at first, ten percent but within a few months half of her earnings. During her spare time, she collected friends' cast-off clothes and brought them to charities around town. What her mother first saw as a noble endeavor turned to worry when Shila not only gave away most of her own clothes but refused to buy new ones when the school year began.

"I would prefer not to," she told her mother when she suggested they shop together for a new wardrobe. "I have enough clothes. I don't need any more."

She foreswore leather and bought only canvas shoes.

"No, thank you," she said when she was offered ice cream for desert. "I'm not using anything that comes from animals—food or clothes or anything else. No make-up."

"What harm is there in drinking milk or eating cheese?"

"You need lactating cows for milk. So they are kept pregnant. Do you know what they do with the male calves that are born?"

Her mother hadn't thought about it before, but now that Shila pointed it out to her, she understood her daughter's reasons for no longer eating any milk product. She had a harder time with Shila's refusal to eat fish, which she had always thought of as creatures with so small a brain as to be hardly more than swimming vegetables. When she pleaded with Shila to at least eat sardines, Shila said that she preferred not to. The offer to buy eggs from free-range chickens was rejected with "Animals have a right not be to be treated as property," a comment presented as so self-evident that no response was possible. She presented a homily about not having pets.

Shila's voice so lacked emotion that Rena reluctantly concluded that her daughter, while a person of great moral conviction and impeccably logical, was a person without passion. Her daughter's problem was that she felt so deeply that she had to shield herself from being overwhelmed by her own feelings. Shila, she thought, was too sensitive, in both senses of that word and, as a result, had become detached, committed and distant all at once.

*R*ena had no answer adequate for Shila when she was asked why they needed four bedrooms in their house. Wouldn't a smaller home do just as well? If a guest ever came to stay overnight, she could share the bedroom with her mother or sleep in the living room. A house this large was an unnecessary indulgence that burdened the environment.

"And we can take the difference between the money from this house and a smaller one and give it to people who don't have anywhere to live. It's wrong for us to stay here."

"But this is where we have lived all these years. It's our home."

"We can live somewhere else. We don't have to be here," Shila said. "Wherever we live is our home."

"But this is where your father and I began, I mean, where we lived—"

"I prefer not to live here any more," Shila said listlessly. "You are being sentimental," she said dryly, a description, not a judgment.

Rena's chest tightened. She closed her eyes briefly before responding. Shila was right: she was being sentimental. But what was wrong with that? Sentiments make life bearable.

"I just want you to be happy," she said.

"I prefer not to."

"Not to what?"

"Be happy. Stupid people are happy. They see all the things that are wrong. All the suffering. The unfairness. And they just do their petty things. But I can't be happy when there is so much misery."

"That doesn't mean that you need to suffer, too," her mother said. "How does you being unhappy make things better?"

"Changing how we *live* will make things better, not how I *feel,*" Shila continued methodically. "My feelings are irrelevant."

Moving, then, wouldn't make Shila happy. Nothing would. But not moving, Rena knew, would make her daughter worse. Besides, she found Shila's logic irrefutable, her thinking implacable. So they moved into an apartment in the city, sold the car, took public transportation to work and school, and contributed the profit from the sale of the house to a shelter for battered women and an animal shelter that didn't euthanize the strays.

Initially, Rena worried about the safety of their new neighborhood. But Shila gave her the statistics: most murders were committed by people who knew the victims; the crime rate was the lowest since statistics were kept; the chances of being in an accident were greater than being mugged on the street.

"And if they did break into the apartment, we don't have anything of value to worry about them taking."

Her mother wondered about where Shila had gotten her facts, but she couldn't disagree with her last point. She was right. They had so few possessions that they owned little more than necessities.

Rena's fears about safety were partially allayed, that is, until Shila stopped riding the bus and began walking, often arriving home long after dark and leaving before dawn in order to get to her class and then work.

"You're taking a bus doesn't keep someone else off," Rena said, anticipating Shila's argument about privilege. "There are enough seats for everyone."

"I gave my monthly pass to a man I saw every night coming home. He has dirty jeans and he falls asleep. He is exhausted. If you saw him, you would know that he needs the pass more than me."

"You're making me sick with worry, Shila. You have to stop."

"You are being irrational," Shila said. "But if you want me to move out so you won't know what time I come in or listen to me, I'll find somewhere else to live."

"I would worry more." And with that Shila continued to live with her mother, who couldn't fall asleep until she heard Shila's key in the door but never said another word to her about walking alone in the dark.

*H*aving graduated from college, Shila began working at a hospital, in the records department. This seemed to be a turn for the better. While Shila's demeanor didn't change, Rena noticed that the circles under her daughter's eyes grew less pronounced and that color returned to her cheeks. Rena knew not to ask after her health, but it was evident that something good was happening—her pallor became not quite a glow but brighter, her sunken cheeks filled out and once again she was using sanitary napkins. No longer anorectic, she gained some substance.

"So how's work?" Rena asked.

"I'm glad to be of some help," was her complete reply.

Was that a smile Rena noticed, a little emotion in her daughter's voice? Rena couldn't keep herself from hoping; she couldn't remember the last time Shila revealed anything resembling delight. Glad that Shila's work provided her with meaning, she didn't dare ask about her love life. Shila had once said that she didn't deserve to be loved—didn't deserve to feel good—when so many children were neglected and beaten, so many women abused.

Rena's hope for her daughter's happiness evaporated when Shila said that she had put herself on a list to donate a kidney.

With the flawless logic of a computer algorithm, Shila presented the argument: people die from renal failure whose lives would otherwise be saved by a transplant; people live normal lives with only one kidney; the chances of dying from donating a kidney is 1 in 4,000; no one's life is more valuable than another; it is obscene to live with something you don't need when by giving it away you can save a life.

"My life isn't worth 4,000 times more than anyone else's," she said. "Every life is as worthy as any other, not more."

"Who is this for? Someone from work? A friend?" she asked. Rena would be reassured if Shila at least admitted to having friends.

"No. For a stranger," she said. "My stipulation is that it go to a poor African American. Some people wait two to three years to get a donor. African Americans wait even longer. Even if I knew someone who needed it, I would give it to a person who has the least a chance of getting one."

"What if it were me?"

"Everyone is the same. Because you are my mother doesn't mean that you are more important than anyone else."

Rena understood Shila's weight gain—she had been too thin to be a donor. Determined to donate her kidney, Shila continued to add fifteen pounds and before the year was out, her kidney was transplanted in a person whose name or condition she didn't want to know. When the hospital sent her a letter of thanks from the donor addressed to her, she refused to read it.

"I didn't do anything special," she said. "I don't deserve any thanks. Everyone ought to do this."

"But they don't," Rena said. "I can't."

"Well, maybe you should."

Rena had come to think that Shila's courage as compassion turned inside out, guilt disguised as conscience. Shila wasn't a moral exemplar but someone who suffered from an illness, she thought, one that benefited others.

*M*issing, the term used by the police, didn't give Rena false hope. She knew that her daughter wasn't missing but gone, that she would never return, even if she could be found, that she was no longer of this material world.

Rena witnessed Shila begin to disappear after the kidney donation. She lost all the weight she had gained prior to the operation.

She now even stopped eating root vegetables because tiny life forms are injured when the plant is pulled up, she explained. She subsisted on fruits, nuts, seeds and a variety of pulses. She would no longer use honey—honey collection is violence against bees, she said.

Although Rena knew the futilety of her words, she expressed her concern to Shila.

"I want to live as lightly as I can," Shila said, "not to cause any harm to any living thing."

Before going to sleep, she shook out her blanket and brushed the sheet so she wouldn't squash bugs while asleep; she emptied the kitchen cabinet of insect repellent, and refused to take antibiotics on the grounds that microbes were living creatures and shouldn't be harmed. She no longer filtered her tap water, for that, too, killed the microscopic creatures that came out of the faucet. She refused to picnic or eat outdoors because the food attracted insects that could be inadvertently crushed underfoot.

"The least amongst us need our care. No life is more important than any other," she said.

"Then take care of your own," Rena said, her hands trembling, losing her temper.

"Anger isn't a useful emotion," Shila said.

Rena wished that Shila showed some emotion, any emotion, any at all. That would be useful.

"You're too attached. You have to let go," Shila said. "Attachment is the source of evil."

In another conversation, Shila told her mother that when she died, she didn't want to be buried, like her father. The next sentence mystified Rena: "Or cremated, either."

"What are you saying, Shila?"

"Do you know how much energy it takes to burn a body?"

No, she didn't, Rena thought, and she didn't want to know.

The first night Shila didn't come home, Rena worried. The second night she received a call from the hospital to inquire after Shila. No one there had seen or heard from her since before the weekend.

"Is she sick?"

"Yes," Rena said ruefully.

Partial remains of a body were found in the woods in a city park near the river. Rats, crows and wild dogs had picked apart the flesh; maggots and worms were feasting on the rest. Rotted but intact clothes lay nearby. There was no violence, the coroner's report said. No force was used. She may have died from starvation, but the coroner couldn't be certain, the police informed Rena.

She left it at that.

KARTIK'S LAST LETTER

DEAR SOMINA,

Today I received your letter from our beautiful home. How I miss it! A day doesn't go by that I'm not thinking about all our uncles and aunties. At night I fall asleep hoping to hear the sound of the frogs and the birds settling in to nest for the night in the reeds. Sometimes I think I hear the brushing of feet in the dust on the path between our houses, thinking that it is company visiting for conversations until it's time to go to sleep, but I am always disappointed that the sounds are only figments in my mind.

I am glad to learn that everyone is fine and healthy, except for the death of Thakur. I hope it was a big funeral for him. The last time I saw him—I can't believe how many years it is already—he was healthy like he always was but already was beginning to be weak with old age. I still think of him with his security guard uniform given to him by the bank. I don't know if I ever told you that I wanted to be like him when I grew up. I'm sorry that I wasn't there to say my final goodbyes to him. He was a good man. I know that. I can remember very well when he came home from his important work in the city and was kind to all the children. But even big men succumb to the toll of time. It is too hard being so far away and not being able to smell the water from the lake and feel the breath of the family on my skin and to say goodbye to people when their time comes.

You tell me you are doing well in your schoolwork. That's good news, indeed. Keep up your marks, Somina. You are a very smart girl. Even when you were little, Auntie Zannat knew you were a clever girl. You were the only daughter she trusted with the fire and with going to the store with a handkerchief full of coins. Of all the children, you are the one she loved most. As your older brother, I can tell you this in all sincerity. I could see that way she took care of your hair and made sure your clothes were clean and bought you shoes even before she bought a pair for herself. I'm sure you know how much she cares about you.

Somina, you make everyone in Daravar proud of what you do. Even from here I know that. You really are the girl tiger of the village. Ggrrrr!!! With your cleverness you will keep the village safe from the devil himself. This is a big job that you have and there is no one better than you to do it. You know the tale. Everyone's grandmother tells it, even to this day. There is even a little book about it, so I think you have read it in school even if you don't remember hearing it at home. I am certain that it is you who it is spoken about. In every generation there is someone who is born to be the leader of the clan and this is you for sure. Maybe you don't know it yet, but I know the prophecy is true. You have always been fierce and smart, just like the tiger that is the protector of our clan, the totem that adorns the doors to the sacred house.

I write to you in answer to your question that you ask again in your letter. When I left, I remember very well the promise I made to you. After awhile, I said, when I had enough money, I would send for you so you too could attend a college here. Now you tell me that you found a college on your own and sent them money from your own savings for your admission's application. This wasn't such a wise idea. I don't know the college you named. It is in a place very far from here—further than even from one end of our country to the other and back again. No one I asked knows of it. It is a mystery college. And when I went to the library to look it up on the Internet, there was something suspicious about it to me. The website looked like it was put together by youngsters who were up to mischief. I'm afraid to tell you that it may not be a real college. There are many scams like this that take advantage of people like us and you have to be very careful not to fall into their traps.

You didn't send them much money, did you? If you sent a money order, it may be very difficult to get it back. But I will see if I can get it back for you. I'll phone them and tell them at the college that I'm a lawyer and I will sue them big time unless they give the money back to my client (I'll call you that). If that doesn't work, I'll write a letter on stationery from a friend of mine who works for a lawyer. Let's hope that this works. I know how hard it is for you to save, and now for you to throw it away in this pulili school is a foolish thing, indeed.

I want to tell you something that I've never told anyone before. Please keep this as a secret between us. No one should ever know. Being here is hard, harder than you can ever imagine. In Daravar, all we see are mountains of money in America, but it isn't like that here. There are mountains of money but they belong to a few people. The mountains are off limits to people like us. If you are lucky, you might be able to get a small mountain, a hill really, maybe more like an anthill, the kind that gets washed away in the rainy season. And that's for very few people who come here wanting to get better things. You may think that I have a house and a car, but I don't have either of those. I live in the bottom of someone else's house and the bed is no better than the one in Daravar. I can't even dream about getting a car. If I had stayed home, I would have a better chance. Here I take two buses to get to my job.

But you do work, I can hear you say. That's true. But it means that I didn't finish college. College is too expensive. The money you sent to the college for the registration, well that is just a small, small part of what it costs every year. I went for a few months and have not been back. You can stop calling me professor, but please, let everyone continue to think that I'm an educated man. To them I can still be Professor Kartik.

I've had many jobs since I got here. Sometimes I quit, they are so boring or it costs me more to get to them than I make in wages. Sometimes I get fired because I am rude to a boss who hates me just because of where I come from or I get lazy. I haven't had one steady job for more than a year. Truth be known, Somina, I've never had a good job. The one I have now is like most of the others. I don't like having to get up in the morning and rush to work. Who in his right mind would want to do that instead of taking breakfast with family and sitting under the eaves when it rains and hear the fronds being beaten? I have to buy all my food. There's no fresh fish. And there's nowhere to grow vegetables.

I'll tell you now that I am lonely almost every day. Here there is no home, only a place to live. At home you are one of many. Here is no many, only you yourself. It would be a very good thing if you were here with me, but there is something else that I need to let you know. The thing I want to tell you is that every time I get my money a few days later it has been eaten by expenses that I never imagined existed. So I did some things that I am ashamed of. I can't even write them down on paper because I am afraid that they will be discovered and I will be in big trouble. Just let me say that if Auntie knew, she would forbid you from seeing me again. My name would be erased from the memory in Daravar, that's how bad it was.

This is what you have to do to survive here and I am not going to let this happen to you. I am going to tell you this story again: When you were born and mother died because you came out backwards, Auntie took you to hospital. She said that your father was dead and now your mother also became late and that if you weren't in hospital, you too would die. She left you there, as an orphan, but only for a short while so you could get strong. She didn't visit you because if she did, they wouldn't let you stay and that would be worse. But while you were there, you got a terrible illness. The news reached our home and when Auntie came to see you, the nurse told her that you had only a short time left for this earth. Everyone made their prayers for you. I remember this well. And I made a solemn promise. I said that if you lived, I would do everything for you like a father. If you came home, I would to make sure that you would grow up to be able to take care of yourself.

I have kept that promise. I paid for doctor's fees since you came home from hospital sick and need special care even to this day. The money from odd jobs in town went for your medicine. I paid the fees for the school for sickly children. And I came to America so that I could make enough to take care of you and Auntie for the rest of your lives. And when I left, you asked for me to send for you and I said, Yes, little sister. I promise.

A promise is solemn and should never be broken. You should never give your word lightly and I didn't. I meant it when I told you that I would make the path clear for you to follow me. But there is another duty that has to be fulfilled. When Auntie took you home, she became your mother. Mothers take care of their children, and she took very good care of you and me, but when children are adults themselves and their parents are old, then it is time for children to take care of them. Auntie is now an old woman and can't be left alone. Who will take care of her if you come to America? What will become of this dear woman? She can't be tossed aside like some useless pot. We owe her that, the two of us, to care for her.

I will continue to send money home but it is to be used for her. Please do everything you can to give her a good home to live in. I trust that you will do this, you are an honorable sister and daughter. Open an account at the bank and I will transfer the money directly to you. Until then, I will send it by Western Union. Use whatever you need to feed yourself and if there is any extra buy yourself a new dress. You are the protector of the home and the tiger. You must be healthy and fierce to do your work.

If things get better for me, someday I will send for you. I don't know when you will get another letter from me. I am going away for a while and it may be difficult for me to write to you. Meanwhile, I remain your loving brother,

Kartik

GIRLS IN PARADISE

"Excuse me. if you don't mind me asking, what do you think of our new slogan, Ms. Tremblay? Do you think it's good? An advertising company in America came up with it."

"What?" Melita, lying on a rattan sun bed, turned her gaze from the turquoise waters. The white sands of the cove beach dazzled in their brightness and the hissing of the palm trees blended with the sound of small waves lapping the shore. Melita looked up and shaded her eyes with her hand. Pillowed clouds drifted across the bright sky over Nyeupe Mchanga Resort and Spa.

It was Kinzoni, the minister she met at the conference the day before, who stood beside her, his shirt radiant in its starched cleanliness.

" 'Paradise Is Yours.' What do you think of it?"

Melita squinted. From under her chaise lounge she recovered her tie-dyed wrap that she bought at a roadside kiosk and covered her legs. She was sorry that she hadn't taken one of the canopied cabanas on the beach instead, feeling exposed in her bathing suit. "It is beautiful," she said.

"Do you mind if I join you?"

She couldn't say no. As Minister of Social Services, in a way she was Kinzoni's guest or at least that of his government. No good could come from rudeness. She didn't want to be with him or any one else from the government. Two days of meetings with these officials was more than she could stand.

"Of course not," Melita said, gesturing to the chair near the umbrella. "Sit." She pulled herself upright. "Please," she added.

It had taken Melita years to accept the practice of staying for a vacation after a work trip. Talking to Kinzoni outside the conference meetings was a line she didn't want to cross.

When Melita began working for the organization that often took her overseas and occasionally to countries that were also holiday destinations, a friend of hers called it hypocritical that some of her colleagues would stay on for a few days for a vacation in the country they were visiting.

Melita initially shared the perception, and perhaps there was something to the charge, but she reconciled herself to the practice. The director at the Committee for the Protection of Girls explained it to her this way: "Look. If you don't take care of yourself, you'll burn out and you won't be good to anyone. You're already there."

"This is a rationalization," Melita protested.

"No. It's the reality," said Axel Beck. He had seen many leave the organization after meeting girls whose arms and lips were cut-off. "You think it's selfish to enjoy yourself. It's the opposite. It's selfish to deprive yourself. You make yourself feel better by denying yourself. But everyone needs some rest and recreation. We don't want martyrs here. They aren't any good to the girls we're working for. You can't make the connection the way you are between your happiness and their hard lives," Axel explained. "You do this work because you think it's important—it is important. Why not enjoy what you can when it's available?"

While CPG's concerns for the rights and welfare of girls were worldwide, the work mainly focused on impoverished countries, so the desire to stay an extra day or two didn't often arise. But some countries, even poor ones, had exclusive resorts that catered to the very wealthy and when the work took the CPG staff there during Canada's long winters, it was hard to resist staying a day or two at one of the world's top 100 resorts, as featured in *Travel and Leisure*. When they stayed in such hotels, they paid for the holiday themselves, finding it affordable since the resorts offered sizeable discounts to personnel from aid agencies and a large part of the expense (the airfare) had already paid for by CPG.

But sometimes the host country extended their stay gratis. The BBC once ran a story condemning the practice. The contretemps over "the perks of compassion" made news for a week, a motion was debated in Parliament, but the story never caught on with a wider audience. The story faded and the board of CPG unanimously refused to adopt a policy condemning it, leaving it to the discretion of the staff to decide on a case-by-case basis whether to take a free room. The board and CPG's director in Toronto trusted their staff's good judgment.

Melita wished they hadn't. She had been uneasy about this trip from the start. She wasn't sure that CPG should participate in a conference sponsored by a government whose human rights record was so abysmal. Her participation seemed like an endorsement, a legitimization, an offering of impunity to men who had done things so unspeakable that Melita decided to never talk about the atrocities outside of work. Some things she needed to leave at the office.

Matters had dramatically improved in this country since the first multi-party election two years before. With the end of the civil war, a semblance of normal life returned. What disconcerted Melita was that the very people who committed the atrocities, the government and the militias, now shared power in a coalition, the rebel leader as vice-president and the former dictator as president. There was still much concern in the international community: the country's most prominent human rights advocate was recently murdered; a newspaper editor was beaten by police; the anti-corruption chief was missing; a dissident politician narrowly escaped from a staged car crash; court cases against the powerful were routinely dismissed. And the plight of girls had barely improved. Although outlawed, in many part of the country FGM was commonplace. The percentage of girls in schools was pitifully low. Former girl soldiers received no treatment in government clinics, as officials denied that girls had ever been used in this way; their problems were of their own making, they said. Arranged marriages, especially for teenage girls like these who became the second or third wives of elderly men, prevailed.

"You play the hand you're dealt," Axel said to Melita. He wanted her to attend the conference as the CPG representative.

"These men are killers," she said.

"Were," he corrected. "We're there to help the girls. The International Criminal Court is there to bring justice. Not us. They prosecute crimes. We help girls. If we can get the government to support our agenda, that's good, isn't it?"

"It's a facade," Melita said. "They'll say whatever they want. Their promises are worthless."

"You won't know that until you get there. Although this is a conference, you're there to get them to agree to our proposed policy changes. At least we have a chance if we can get them to agree to this publicly."

"Do you really believe that, Axel, that they're serious about this? Why do you think they can be trusted? They'll say anything, then do what they want."

Money intended for good causes often found its way into the pockets of officially sanctioned thieves and laws that sounded good on paper were never enforced. This was standard fare. And Melita anticipated Axel's answer, as she often gave it to newer employees herself: look at the countries that have moved from genocide to models of good governance; terrorists who wind up receiving peace prizes; former war zones that are featured as travel destinations. The world is unpredictable. Besides—the clincher—do you have a better plan?

This trip was different, though. Never before had CPG agreed to participate in a conference sponsored by those who, it was rumored, were awaiting indictments by an international court for crimes against humanity.

Making Melita's decision more difficult was that while staff from other European NGOs would be present, she was the sole representative from her organization. Since the worldwide economic collapse, Axel couldn't justify sending more than one person to this meeting. The organization had been forced to shut more than a dozen programs. Only Axel was more senior than Melita and he was needed in the main office to manage the deteriorating finances and to help stave off further shutdowns and redundancies.

Melita was going to have to make the trip herself.

$\mathcal{A}$t the conclusion of the meeting, other NGO staff departed Nyeupe Mchanga that evening on flights to London and Berlin, leaving Melita alone with a dozen other vacationers, including Chiku, a world-famous entertainer who stayed to herself, behind the wall of a villa larger than Melita's suburban bungalow in Richmond Hill.

"I hope you found the conference productive," Kinzoni said as he lowered himself onto the chair. He motioned to a waiter. Melita asked for coconut water. "Don't you drink?" Kinzoni ordered a pint of pilsner and a plate of beef samosas.

Melita said, leaving it ambiguous as to what she was responding to, "No." She had learned how to be diplomatic.

" 'Paradise Is Yours.' I think it's quite good," Kinzoni said in a self-satisfied manner. "The Ministry of Tourism is going to launch a campaign in Europe and North America soon. We think there's a niche for us in the upscale market. This is what we have to sell to the world. I know it isn't what many think today. But it is paradise." Kinzoni smacked his lips, then wiped the grease with a linen serviette. "Won't you have one?"

"No, thank you." She couldn't bring herself to take anything from a plate that he had touched. She cradled the green coconut in her hands and sipped the water through a straw. No one was on the beach, an exclusive preserve for guests.

"I have great hopes for this country." He held his glass up in front of him, looked at the sparkling amber.

"Everyone wants the best."

"There's much to be done."

Melita turned away from Kinzoni.

"Well, I see that you would like to be alone. I won't disturb you any more."

"No, please . . ."

"We're all exhausted, I'm sure, Ms. Tremblay. These meetings can be very tiring, indeed." He put his beer glass on the table and stood up. "Tonight there's a reception for some of our special guests. I hope you can make it. You'll have to try the samosas there."

"I'll do my best, Mr. Kinzoni. Thank you for the kind offer."

Melita returned to her villa, the sitting room full of furniture carved from driftwood and piles of woven baskets, the rosewood floor polished to sheen, and at the foot of the bed were batik cloths. The mahogany bowl had been refilled with fresh fruit and newly cut flowers were placed next to the bed. She took a shower in the outdoor enclosure and fell asleep in the glow of the canvas panel walls of the room illuminated by the afternoon sun.

Her plan to dine alone that night was overturned when she read the card in the vellum envelope that had been slipped under her door. The invitation, signed by President Ambrose Obengi, respectfully requested her presence for dinner. Melita felt angered but also flattered by the personal summons. Meetings with heads of state were rare and it was always Axel who represented CPG.

Acknowledging to herself that she had no choice but to accept the invitation, she realized that the only clothes she had with her were those she had brought for a meeting in the tropics—slacks, blouses and sandals. She didn't have a dress or a pair of high heels; she had no make-up, no jewelry other than another pair of earrings. And there wasn't anywhere to purchase clothing. Nyeupe Mchanga didn't yet have a gift shop.

What was she thinking, how superficial could she be, being concerned about what she would wear to meet a brutal man? Melita thought about the girls whose welfare she was there to represent and now felt that it was right that she would meet the president in what for her were her work clothes after all. If his was a bespoke suit from a shop on Savile Row, she could wear off-the-rack pants from a Richmond Hill mall.

"Ah, how nice of you to come," Kinzoni said when Melita walked onto a patio overflowing with hibiscus and wild ginger. "A glass of wine for you? No, I'm sorry. I forgot you don't drink."

"As a matter of principle, before dinner," she said. She needed something to calm her nerves.

He snapped his fingers and ordered her a glass of Chablis.

"The President is down for a meeting with his political party. This is his home constituency. So he isn't here on state affairs."

Melita couldn't take her eyes off the only other woman in the room.

"Have you met her before?" Kinzoni asked, catching Melita's gaze. "Her father is from this district. Her mother is from China."

"A very beautiful woman."

Kinzoni laughed.

"For some, the most beautiful in the world."

"Does she live here?" Melita asked in a voice barely audible.

Kinzoni laughed again.

"She always stays at Nyeupe Mchanga when she returns home. If I am not mistaken, her primary home is in Rome. She is a woman of the world." Kinzoni looked at Melita. "You don't recognize her?"

"Should I?"

"It's Chiku." The film star, supermodel, singer, TV show-host, the most recognized female face in the world, the humanitarian. The president's goddaughter.

A tall man with deep creases in his forehead and wearing glasses, his close-cropped hair graying, walked over to Chiku. They talked briefly. He then took a box from an aide at his side, opened it and fastened a necklace of sapphires and white and blue diamonds around Chiku's neck. She kissed him on the cheek. The president then left the room, nodding to Melita as he passed her by and everyone followed except for Chiku and Melita who remained alone with the waitstaff. Perhaps this was an opportunity to recruit a celebrity as a spokesperson for CPG, something that had been discussed at meetings in Toronto, as a way of attracting more funding.

Chiku acknowledged Melita with a raised eye and began to walk toward her.

Melita stared at the necklace that glittered in the candlelight. She estimated how many schools and clinics such a necklace could buy, how many other extraordinary pieces of jewelry Chiku must own, how many more illicit gems President Ambrose Obengi stashed in vaults around the world.

Chiku was about to greet her when Melita, avoiding the superstar's gaze, walked past her with a cursory nod and returned to her room. She wouldn't tell Axel about Chiku. She knows that he would have approached Chiku to get her endorsement for the organization. Sadly, this is what fundraising has come to. Without a celebrity's name, CPG was just another do-good NGO, one of thousands, one that may well close its doors in the near future.

On the walk back to her villa, under armed guard to protect her against marauding wildlife, Melita already regretted her snubbing Chiku. It's the girls, the girls, she said to herself. It's not me that matters but them.

Hardly settled in her room, Melita received another invitation: once again a handwritten invitation from the president requested her presence, this time in his villa.

"He is expecting you now," the solider said, standing in the doorway. "Please come with me."

Had Chiku complained to her godfather about her rudeness? Melita wondered. Before leaving her room, she texted Axel to tell him about the situation, in case she, too, disappeared.

"Be careful," he texted back.

"Ms. Tremblay," the president addressed Melita, "please sit down." He signaled his bodyguard to leave. This villa was twice the size of hers. The doors to the wrap-around patio were open. She could hear the surf, the palm leaves, the insects. President Obengi sat upright on a large chair, a glass of Scotch whiskey next to him and beside that a bowl of tropical fruits, a mango peel curled on a plate.

"Johnny Walker Blue Label," he said, pointing to the bottle in a silk-lined box. "Can I offer you some? No, my minister told me that you don't drink."

The president had removed his suit jacket and tie and sat with his bare feet crossed in front of him. "Minister Kinzoni told me about you and the conference these last couple of days. He said that he was impressed with you. You've asked for many things."

"All in the name of justice for girls, Mr. President. Nothing more"

"Quite so," he said softly. "I looked at the proposals you have made. They seem quite reasonable to me." When he removed his glasses to rub his eyes, Melita noticed his sclera were red. The vigor of his voice belied the beleaguered and haggard look that revealed itself in this room bright with lights. "The future of our country is good. All indicators are positive and would have been much better if not for the worldwide recession." He poured himself another glass of Scotch whiskey. "Would you rather have something else instead? Whatever you want."

"Nothing, thank you," she said. Her heart was beating quickly and she could hardly catch her breath.

"Why did you want to see me, Mr. President?"

"I like your proposals. They are eminently sane. Reasonable. I want to tell you that some of them I will propose to Parliament immediately. We want to bring our country into line with the most advanced."

He talked about changes in inheritance, outlawing forced marriages, ensuring that schools admit an equal number of girls.

"I'm hungry, Ms. Tremblay. Please join me." He walked to a table set with cold lobster. "When I was a child, we used to throw these back into the water," he said, putting on a bib. "They were just garbage that we picked up with the fish we were really looking for." He stopped and twisted off the legs and pried out the meat with a claw. "Until we learned that you considered these a delicacy. You are right. And we have the best." He picked up the two-pound lobster and cracked the shell with a hammer. "Are you sure you don't want to join me?" President Obengi grabbed the lobster. "The best part," he said, as he twisted the meat loose and pushed it through the tail.

"Whatever is policy, I promise you that soon they will be law. And, I assure you, it will be more than words. I personally will stand behind each of the provisions."

Melita's mouth was dry. Her eyes were wide.

"Is this why you wanted to see me?" she asked. "It is good news. CPG will be happy to see this when it becomes law."

"Of course you have good reason to doubt our sincerity." He wiped his mouth. He poured a glass of wine, finishing the bottle of Chardonnay. "Come, join me on the patio. It is a beautiful night. Paradise is yours tonight, Ms. Tremblay."

She tensed her body as he took her by the elbow to lead her outside.

"That's a constellation you can't see where you come from," Obengi said. "But you have more visible stars in the Canadian sky. It is the way the Earth tilts into the Milky Way. You look into it, we are facing the other way." Leaning on the rail, he made no move to touch her. He rubbed his forehead with his thumb. "There's so much to be done. So much pain to be undone." He paused. "I want to make it right. I have a lot of money, Ms. Tremblay. I want to put it to use. So I want to make you a proposition."

When Obengi turned to look at her, Melita nearly bolted into the dark below the patio.

"I want to pledge part of my fortune to you. To CPG, that is. I asked my government to do a little research and Mr. Kinzoni has convinced me that of all the work being done to rehabilitate girls, yours is doing the best job." He paused. "And that you desperately need money to stay afloat." He told her the annual deficit CPG was running. The figures sounded about right to Melita. As an NGO, the Committee for the Protection of Girls' finances was a matter of public record, easily accessible on the Internet. "My budget office tells me that you don't have more than a couple of years to turn it around."

The president moved closer to her.

"What is it, Ms. Tremblay? There's no reason to be afraid. Don't believe the stories you read. I'm a harmless person."

"The pledge, Mr. President?" Melita was hyper-ventilating. "What's is this pledge you want to make?"

"Calm down, please. Take a seat." Obengi pulled over an armchair for her. Melita continued to stand. "I will make personal donations—my own money, Ms. Tremblay, my own money—to support every project CPG wants to build here. I will personally pay for them entirely. No cost to your organization. The money won't come from my government."

The president said that CPG could pick the projects and train the staff. "I do have a requirement. It is that all the personnel must be local, Ms. Tremblay. No expatriates on the ground. You understand."

"Who will supervise the programs?"

"These are CPG's. You have the expertise. This is all I insist upon, that all employees here be locals." He explained that, however, there was a limit to his largesse. "But $10 million a year—each year—can go a long way, I should think," he said, pleased with himself. "But if you should ever need more, you can always ask." He handed Melita an envelope. "This is the first year's contribution." He laughed again and put his hand on top of hers. "If I were in your country, I would have a big tax deduction."

She looked at the unsealed envelope with the presidential seal and regained her ability to speak.

"So you are making a donation to CPG," is all that she managed to say.

"Indeed. I can think of no better way a providing a legacy."

"This is . . . very generous," Melita fumbled.

"Some benefactors have to be asked to have their names on buildings and such. But you never thought that I would agree."

"You want you name on . . .?"

"The CPG Ambrose Obengi Centers. Nothing more. It is as I stated. You decide the program. You decide where to establish centers. I'll secure the land for you. You decide how many centers to build. There's no limit. I am happy to make the gift. I can see no end to it."

Even if he is indicted? Even if his assets are seized? Even if he is imprisoned by The Hague? And what if CPG continued to receive the grant, year after year, erecting centers in his name, centers that make better the lives of the girls of paradise?

Melita thought about this on the plane home to Toronto. And she thought about his last gesture, when he handed her a purse made of banana leaves.

"And a little gift for you in making this a reality. Do with it as you please. Don't worry. No one will bother you at customs control. You have my word."

At the check-in at the airport she was told that she had been up-graded to first-class and now in the privacy of her sleeper seat she opened the packet again and poured the fistful of uncut gems in her palm. In the hiss of the plane, she fingered the stones like prayer beads.

The steward startled Melita. "Can I get you anything, madam?"

"I'm fine," she said unconvincingly.

Before landing, the crew, as Melita had seen on many flights before, requested donations in foreign currencies that travelers may not yet have converted to Canadian dollars be given to a charity this time for children with cerebral palsy. The stewards came up the aisle holding plastic bags in front of them.

Melita tied the gems in a paper napkin and when a steward reached her row, she cupped her hand so he couldn't see the napkin she dropped into the plastic bag.

"Thank you for your donation," he said.

"Thank you for caring," she responded.

THE TRAIN TO AMSTERDAM

$\mathcal{W}$HILE MANY AUSTRIANS SUPPORTED A MERGER with Germany, just as many opposed it. The matter of converting Austria into a region of Germany was so divisive that the country's chancellor, Kurt Schuschnigg, scheduled a referendum for March 13th to let the populace decide, once and for all, whether the Austrian people should become German citizens.

No one in Danilo Altman's family expected matters to take the sudden turn that it did.

"The Austrian people are too sensible," Danilo said at the dinner table, as his wife and son listened. "I talked to people in my factory. No one wants union with the lunatics in Berlin. I'm telling you, we will be safe."

"Oh, Danilo," his wife responded. "They only tell you what they know you want to hear. You are their boss, after all. But you see the rallies. They can't wait . . ."

"And there are rallies against unification, too, Vera. Just as many. More."

A large chandelier hung over the mahogany table, under which was a dark red Persian rug.

"But it won't be up to us. Germany will get what it wants, Poppa," Rudolph said. "*Heim ins Reich.* Home into the Empire. That's what I hear in gymnasium. Home into the Empire. Home into the Empire. The boys at school, they're all in favor of it. They come to school in their uniforms. They can't wait to become Germans. My schoolmates are mad for it."

"That's why they're still schoolboys, Rudolph, and why the chancellor has excluded anyone younger than 24 from participating in the plebiscite."

"They may be schoolboys but they make a lot of noise. But it's not just them. Everyone favors pan-Germany."

"Not everyone, Rudolph. Some people just say this but they don't really mean it. You'll see when they count the votes. In three days it will be settled," Danilo said, as his voice grew louder. "I tell you, your schoolmates don't know what the people really want. They're only speaking as children."

Danilo picked up his glass of Blaufränkisch, twirled the wine and sniffed. With a smile he said, "When they know the difference between good wine and bad, then they can speak." He took a sip. "Take some, Rudolph," he said, leaning across the table to pour some in his son's water glass. "I know. They talk to me in my factory. They come into my office and tell me. They respect me."

"What do they tell you, Danilo?" Vera interjected. "They'll tell you what you want to hear. Behind your back they may be saying something else. You have Nazis working for you."

"And communists and socialists and Christian Socialists. Everyone works for me. Except anarchists."

"You can't trust any of them," she said.

"How can you live your life without trusting people? I have had no problems with my workers, Vera. You know that. They are loyal. But maybe the women you associate with are different. What do you hear?" Danilo asked his wife.

"You see it for yourself. They are in love with Hitler. Mention his name and they swoon. They have fallen in love with a lunatic and there is no reasoning with them. Just like the German women. No different. They're lovesick. Besides," Vera added, "Hitler has already renounced the referendum as a fraud. He won't accept anything but *Anschluss.*"

"So what do you think he will do? Invade? We are protected by international treaties," he said emphatically.

"He doesn't care about treaties or laws." Vera looked at her husband with her soft blue eyes. "And when he comes, he'll be welcomed like a returning hero. You'll see."

"He may be a buffoon, Vera, but he isn't an idiot. He won't risk an international reaction. It doesn't matter that these boys call out his name or the women wet their pants. He seeks acceptance by civilized people—Great Britain and France. It's their opinions that matter to him." Danilo turned to his son. "What do you think, Rudolph?"

"I think it won't make difference one way or the other," Rudolph responded heatedly. "We're already a fascist state."

"But not Nazi!"

"We may as well be."

"Not Nazis!" Danilo knocked over his wine glass and the white tablecloth stained red. "I'm sorry, Vera. I'll buy you another on the way home from the factory tomorrow. I'm sorry, Rudolph.

Forgive me. I shouldn't lose my temper. There isn't enough level-headedness as it is." Danilo recomposed himself. He continued as though conducting a seminar about an important but mostly theoretical subject. "What I mean to say is that democracy will return one day. Our local Nazis—I know some. Of course. They are in my factory, too. Take Michael Knauss, for example. He is a fine boy. I've known him since he was little. He father used to work for me, too."

"You see one thing at work. I am sure he is fine there. But I've seen him on the streets, Danilo," Vera said. "He wears the Nazi youth uniform and shouts Hitler's name and spits on Jews."

"I can't believe this, Vera. He wouldn't do such a thing. He's always polite and well-behaved."

"He's the head of the Nazi Youth Corps, Poppa," Rudolph interrupted. "Don't you know this? It's no secret. He's a bully, like all the youth corps."

"In the factory he is a good worker. I've never had trouble with him. He's young, like you, Rudolph. Some young people do foolish things." Danilo looked down at the table. Then he slowly said, "Some day we'll all regain our good senses." He patted the wet tablecloth with his napkin and lifted his head. "Agreed?" Danilo filled his glass to the top, held it up and said, "To a better tomorrow."

"May it be so."

*T*omorrow was, in fact, worse. Hitler wasn't going to wait any longer to annex Austria and that morning demanded that by the end of the day Kurt Schuschnigg relinquish power to the German Worker's Party, an Austrian group that recognized Hitler as the Fuhrer. If the chancellor refused, Germany would immediately send in its troops to restore order.

Schools were shut as soon as the students heard the German Chancellor's remarks; Nazis and their supporters stormed out of Altman Metalworks, and Danilo was forced to close its doors before noon.

The Altmans listened to *Radio Wien* broadcast bulletins from Vienna.

"The clown is just bluffing," Danilo said calmly. "He won't provoke England. He is clever but not stupid."

Rudolph listened to his father's anodyne and sat silently running his fingers through his thick black hair. His neck turned damp with sweat. The newscasts were frantic and dire; they were confused and contradictory.

Rapping on the front door startled the family.

"Don't get up!" Vera said. She gripped Danilo's right hand in hers.

"It's all right," Danilo assured her as he gently pried her hand from the top of his. "There's nothing to worry about. What do you expect me to do, Vera? We can't refuse to answer. It may be someone who needs us."

When Danilo opened the door, he was greeted with "Heil," accompanied by an outstretched right arm.

"Knauss? Why . . . What . . .?" Danilo stumbled over his words, seeing, for the first time, his young employee wearing a Hitler-Youth uniform. Danilo glanced at the swastika band wrapped around the left sleeve of Knauss's jacket, a silver chain looped from the lapel to the breast pocket.

"Let me in," Knauss said. "I want to talk to you."

Danilo could feel Vera's and Rudolph's cold silence behind him.

"Mr. Altman!" he insisted. Knauss removed his cap and looked up into Danilo's eyes.

"Can't this wait? I'll talk to you tomorrow in my office." Danilo, much bigger than Knauss who was thirty years his junior, blocked the doorway. "This isn't a good time to see me."

"I insist, Mr. Altman," Knauss said as he placed his free hand on the doorjamb and thrust the toe of his left boot on the doorsill.

"Vera," Danilo called to his wife. "We have a guest. Rudolph. Turn off the radio." Danilo stepped aside for the youth leader. "Please, Rudolph."

Rudolph rose from the settee.

"Ask him to stay, Mr. Altman," Knauss said. "This is for him, too."

Knauss's impertinence and Danilo's deference unnerved Rudolph. He stood next to his mother, who remained seated on the button-tufted sofa.

"Let me get to the point," Knauss said formally. "You know the news from Vienna."

"Of course. We are listening to the radio," Danilo replied.

"There's more you need to know." Knauss stood stiffly, holding his cap behind his back. "In my office I have information that isn't yet public. I know for certain that the German army will be in Austria within days."

"Rumors."

"No, Mr. Altman. Maybe that is what you wish. The reality is that by the end of the week Austria and German will be gloriously reunited."

"And why are you telling me this, may I ask?"

"Mr. Altman," Knauss said, "you have been very good to me at the Metalworks. When my father was sick, you paid his medical bills. You helped with the funeral. My mother appreciates the pension you provide her. You are a good man, Mr. Altman. You have been kind and generous to all your employees at Metalworks. I have no ill wishes for you. But it is unfortunate that you aren't one of us. You must know that your time here is over."

"Nazis won't win . . ."

"You are mistaken. We have already won. Tomorrow belongs to us, Mr. Altman."

"Why are you here, Michael?"

"I don't want you or your family to come to harm. I can give you safe passage to The Netherlands. From there you can make your way to England."

Danilo's face flushed bright red. Beads of sweat formed on his forehead. "Get out!" Danilo shouted. "Do you think I am such a coward that I will give my factory to you? That I will abandon my house because you threaten me?"

"Please, Mr. Altman. Take this in the spirit I am offering it." Knauss's eyes softened. Danilo could see the boy he once knew. Knauss turned cold again. "I am not threatening you but warning you and giving you the opportunity for you to save your family. I know the plans made in Berlin that you can't even imagine. Think about it. After this week it may be too late."

"I'm no fool, Michael. And I'm not a coward. I'm not going anywhere. I won't run away."

Michael Knauss stood with his legs wide apart and his hands still folded behind his back.

"When my father had no work, your father gave him a job. And you have been very good to all of us at the Metalworks. All the workers appreciate your generosity. Whenever there has been a sacrifice to make, you have made it with us. On this there is no disagreement amongst fascists, socialists or communists. I want to repay my family's debt to yours."

Danilo tried to see beyond the uniform, the stone blue coldness in the eyes.

"This is the best I can do, Mr. Altman," Knauss said. "One at a time. One at a time." He handed Danilo a business-size envelope. "This is what he needs."

Danilo took the packet of papers. He opened the flap and saw a passport with his son's name on it.

"I will meet Rudolph at the train station on Sunday morning. You and Mrs. Altman must stay home. I'll accompany him on the train to Amsterdam. I promise you, I'll make certain that he will get there and I will see him through immigration."

"This is madness."

"It is an opportunity, Mr. Altman."

Danilo looked at the passport.

"How can I trust you, Michael?"

"Listen to the news tomorrow. If it is as I say, then you know I am telling the truth. Mr. Altman," he said, lowering his voice. "Has my family ever done harm to you?"

Knauss explained his plan: first get Rudolph out of Austria safely, then Mrs. Altman, and finally Danilo. He couldn't get all the documents ready at one time without arousing suspicion. He had prepared Rudolph's documents and needed time to get the others in order.

*A*fter listening to *Radio Wien* the following day—streets in Vienna overrun with mobs deliriously waiting for Hitler, Jews dragged from cars; Jewish-looking pedestrians beaten; torahs torn from the alcoves of synagogues; department stores and apartments of Jews looted; one correspondent reported that rabbis were being made to clean toilets with their prayer shawls.

What the Altmans couldn't know was that this was only the beginning and that in less than six months nearly all of Austria's synagogues would be destroyed, thousands of homes and businesses demolished and its Jewish citizens rounded up for deportation.

Danilo and Vera didn't strictly follow Michael's directions. They stood near the station as the two young men boarded the soot-covered carriage of the train bound for Amsterdam. They had said their good-byes at the house and instructed Rudolph not to turn around at the station. They would watch from a distance, they told him, and "if Michael does anything funny," Danilo said, "I will get you," and nothing did happen. The engine heaved and hissed and the train slowly disappeared into the valley of the forested mountain behind the city.

When Michael returned from Amsterdam, he assured the Altmans that all had gone well. He had walked with their son as far as immigration and needed to leave him there. He watched until he saw Rudolph pass through the barrier and merge with the crowd on the other side, certain that he was safely in The Netherlands.

"Yes, he called yesterday to tell us that he arrived safely and that you took good care of him," Vera said.

"I'll have your papers in a month, Mrs. Altman," Michael said curtly.

Five months later, Danilo watched his wife board the train with his former employee, now the head of the Nazi Youth for the province.

Rudolph and his mother waited in Amsterdam for Danilo. After the success of spiriting out two family members, they were certain that Danilo would join them. But he never arrived. Neither remembers when they gave up hope. It must have been some time before they emigrated from Holland to the United States, before the German occupation and the deportation of Jews from that nation.

Long after his mother's death, Rudy Altman returned to Austria from their New York home to try to find out his father's fate.

The city of his boyhood was gone, razed by Allied bombings and urban renewal. The Altman house was replaced by a shopping center catering to skiers in the nearby resort. A new, larger train station stood in place of the wooden structure. There was no trace of the Altman Metalworks factory; it had been targeted in a B-17 raid because it was manufacturing munitions. Now there was a park landscaped with mountain flora, its playground filled with children, the pitch occupied by boys his age when he left.

Unlike some other countries, there was no memorial book for Austrian victims of the Holocaust for Rudy to consult. But a manifest at city hall indicated that Danilo Altman was amongst deportees to Stutthof, the concentration camp near Danzig, the place where soap was produced from human fat.

Through a series of inquiries to historical associations in

Vienna, Rudy learned that in 1940 Michael Knauss became an officer in the *SS-Totenkopfverbande* and had been stationed near his home, in the Austrian concentration camp, Mauthausen-Gusen, where he supervised slave laborers at the granite quarry. The last mention of Knauss on the camp roster was in 1944. When the camp was liberated, Knauss wasn't amongst the Nazis captured by the Allies. There was no record of a transfer from the camp before this date, no death certificate could be located. It was as though he had dissolved, just like Danilo Altman in Poland.

Each spring, as the *yahrzeit* candles burn for 24 hours in memory of his parents, Rudy looks at the only visual record he has of his parents, their wedding photo that his mother brought with her from Austria. The lighting of the candles causes Rudy to think about Knauss, the young man with him on the train to Amsterdam who played solitaire for the entire trip, then, without a word, patted him on his shoulder as he walked through Central Station and when leaving, his passport stamped and his visa accepted, gave him a stiff-armed salute good-bye.

BLACK ICE

CHANIA BARELY KNEW HER OLDER COUSIN. AL-though their homes were less than a hundred miles apart, the massif that loomed east of the city made visiting difficult between them. Landslides often closed the single, sinuous road across the snow-capped mountain to the high plateau beyond and in winter the road was impassable.

What Chania liked best about her visits to her uncle's sprawling ranch were the long-maned ponies. The cousins seldom talked, as he was a half-dozen years older than she and he preferred the company of adults.

Two years ago, when Chania was a sophomore in high school, Pandin disappeared. The police never found his body and the case officially remained opened, but everyone knew what had happened: the chairman of the Bhara Human Rights Committee had been abducted and likely murdered.

This visit by Uncle Rohr and Aunt Hajip to Chania's apartment in the city was the first time since Pandin's disappearance that she and her mother had seen them.

"I don't care that you want to hang out with your friends, Chania," Khadroma said. "They are your uncle and aunt."

"But I have tickets for a concert with my friends," Chania told her mother. "We made these plans week ago. I can't let them down."

"Yes, you can. And you will."

Chania had always been headstrong. From the moment she entered school, teachers complained about her boisterousness, inability to sit still, rudeness and unwillingness to follow directions. She didn't hesitate to talk back to teachers. Chania blamed the teachers for treating her unfairly. They were stupid jerks, she said. Chania used other epithets and curses that Khadroma had never heard before. Despite her disdain for school, Chania excelled on the national examinations, particularly in mathematics, and was admitted to high school.

"Sometimes I think you are too smart for your own good," Khadroma chided her. "You need to learn to respect people, even if you don't like them or disagree with them. You have to get along. Some day you will get yourself in big trouble."

"They're bigots. They humiliate me. They don't call on me when I raise my hand. The teacher baited me. He said I needed to bathe and called me a termite in front of the whole class. So I called him a ferret."

Khadroma was horrified but couldn't help but laugh, and then caught herself. Prejudice against Bharas was endemic and had existed as long as anyone remembered. In the last few years, though, it had become a drumbeat, expressed with impunity. Teachers, commentators and ordinary people felt free to say that Bharas were sneaky, aggressive, clever, abrasive, dirty, obnoxious, untrustworthy, clannish, thickheaded and self-centered.

"A mangy ferret. That's what I called him."

Khadroma knew that Chania was the only Bhara in the classroom and her teachers constantly reminded her of it.

"But don't use their pettiness as an excuse. You will never succeed in life with a chip on your shoulder. You are bigger than they are. They can only make you feel small if you let them. It was the same with your father and me when we were in school. That's just the way it is."

"I'm not like you. I'm not going . . ."

"Yes. You are going to finish school. How else will get by in life? You're going to write a letter of apology and that's the end of it. When you get a job, then you'll see what the real world is like. You'll look back on this as the best time of your life."

"Anything is better than school!"

"You are looking very pretty today," Aunt Hajip said.

"You've really grown-up since we last saw you. Like a young woman. I like what you've done to your hair." Hajip leaned over and stroked Chania's thick hair. "How are you, my dear?"

"As well as can be expected," Chania answered.

"She was expelled from school." Khadroma looked at her daughter from across the room. Chania's arms were folded across her chest. "For talking back to a teacher."

"He should be talked back to," Chania said. "He's a Bhara hater."

Rohr took his wife's hand. With his free hand he brushed back a wisp of his own hair.

"Chania . . ." Khadroma began.

"It's alright, Khadroma. She's right. Things are getting worse." Rohr stopped himself as Hajip squeezed his hand.

"She's annoyed because she wants to go to a show today," Khadroma explained. "I told her that she had to visit with you."

"Why shouldn't she go? That's what girls are supposed to do at her age," Aunt Hajip said. "Here, Chania." She handed her niece an envelope. "This is a little gift from your uncle and me. If it's OK with you, Hajip, let her enjoy herself today. Buy yourself something beautiful. Don't worry, Khadroma. We'll still be here when she returns and she'll show us what she's bought."

Chania kissed her aunt on the cheek and nodded her head in thanks.

"That girl gives me headaches sometimes," Khadroma said when Chania left, then caught herself, thinking about her in-laws' sorrow.

"She just a teenager," Hajip said.

"We have something to tell you, Khadroma," Rohr said, leaning closer in. "We didn't want to talk about it in front of the girl." He took a sip of potent pistachio liqueur from a tiny, sculpted glass. "Hajip and I have decided that we are leaving."

"The ranch? Are you retiring?"

"Our property is being taken over by the government." He wiped his sticky hands with the napkin. "We've been given notice. They say it is for a waterway. Who knows? What's the difference? It's only an excuse. We're not wanted here. We have a year to leave. They've offered us a pittance of what the houses, livestock and land are worth."

"But we have enough savings," Hajip added before Khadroma could interject. "Rohr has been putting money in a foreign account. We will use what we've saved."

Khadroma was stunned. The family had been farming the same land for generations. "What are you going to do?"

"We have enough money to start over. Start over some place new. Away from here," Hajip said. "We're getting old. Maybe we'll just retire."

"Our passports are in order. We're going to seek residence in another country."

Khadroma mouth fell open and she dropped her plum pastry on the carpet.

"We've made inquiries. There are Bharas there who will help us settle."

Hajip said, "We want you to come with us."

Khadroma was at a loss for words. She leaned against her chair.

"Go with you? I can't do that," she finally said. "I can't go just like that."

"There's a year. Long enough. And why not, Khadroma? Why not leave? There's nothing here for you."

"Chania."

"Of course. We mean for both of you."

Khadroma walked to the kitchen and returned with a cup of coffee.

"No, no. It's out of the question. For one, I am too old to learn a new language," Khadroma said "I can't start over again."

"I am already learning myself," Rohr said. "Hajip and I have bought CDs that we listen to. It isn't very hard, Khadroma."

"You've always been smarter than me," she said.

"Stop, Khadroma. You can do it. Stay with us," Hajip said. "Soon Chania will be out of the home. She'll be on her own, and then it will be too late. Then what, if you stay here? You'll be alone. That wouldn't be good."

Khadroma had managed well enough since her husband died, she said. There was enough money from the life insurance policy to modestly support them for the rest of their lives.

"Come, come. We are too worried about you. Do you think you will be left alone? If they can take away my ranch, how safe do you think you will be?"

Khadroma always trusted Rohr's judgment. He understood the world far better than she, she thought.

"I will talk to Chania about it," she conceded.

She did, after Rohr and Hajip left after breakfast the next day. Khadroma told Chania what Uncle and Aunt had said: they were afraid that there was no future here for Bharas and they should consider leaving with them.

Chania dismissed the idea.

"I'm just starting my life. I graduate in two months. I already have a job. They will make me full-time when I graduate."

"You can start somewhere else, someplace better."

"Maybe *you* don't have friends," she added cruelly. "But I have. I'm not leaving them."

Chania was right. Neighbors in the apartment house were all Bhara, but she never opened her heart to one. Yet there were things more important than friends, Khadroma thought: all her memories—herself—were planted in this place; tending to her husband's grave; not conceding to fear. But none were more important than life itself or her daughter's future. The future trumped the past.

"You will make new friends, Chania. You're young," Khadroma said.

"And you are thinking like an old woman. The world isn't like that any more. That's history."

"No. It's reality. You know what it's like in school."

"They're just the teachers. Old people. My friends aren't like that. My manager is very nice to me."

Khadroma wanted to be persuaded by her daughter and she let herself be.

But Rohr continued to call Khadroma. "For Chania's sake. Please."

"She doesn't want to leave," Khadroma explained. "Her life is here. I won't leave without her. She is still a teenager. She isn't as smart as she thinks."

"I am telling you. No good will come of staying put," he said. "The fires will only get worse and no one will be able to control them. Mark my words. This is only the beginning of the end. Tell her she must leave with you."

*R*ohr's predictions seemed accurate when, the following year, dozens of Bharas died in a community center locked from the outside, choking to death from the fumes and smoke of gasoline bombs thrown through windows. In the west, a tour bus of Bharas was hijacked and all the passengers murdered.

Then there was a lull—no more mass killings, only individual attacks in markets, school grounds and sports arenas. Internet blogs continued to stoke resentment against those "eating unseen at the nation's foundation." National newspapers and TV broadcasts condemned the violence; the president expressed his dismay. ('Hypocrite,' Khadroma muttered to herself.) She wished that Rohr was wrong and that the fires were finally quenched and the country would be stronger from the burnings—like saplings and fresh grass, some said, that sprouts after the periodic clearing of cedars forests and weedy meadows by periodic fires.

So, too, Chania believed, when she thought about such things at all, one year out of high school and enjoying her work and having gotten a promotion and pay raise.

But when Chania told Khadroma that she was engaged, her mother was irate.

"I don't approve," she said. "How do you expect me to approve?"

"What wrong with Sopori?"

"What's wrong with him? How do I know if there is anything wrong with him? I can't say if he is fine or not. I have never met the boy. But I know enough to disapprove."

"I want to bring him home, but you don't want me to. I'll bring him here tomorrow . . ."

"No," Khadroma hissed, "He's not a Bhara. I'm not going to have his kind in my home. Do you understand me, Chania?" Khadroma bit her lower lip, her eyes watering with rage. She glowered at her daughter. "We have enough trouble as it is."

"Fine," Chania said curtly. "Fine, then. You won't meet him."

"I want you to stop seeing him, Chania. Find another boy."

Khadroma met Sopori unexpectedly, several months later,

when she returned home from shopping and found Sopori and Chania on the living room sofa.

Sopori grabbed his shirt, fumbling with the buttons as he hurriedly put it on.

"This is Sopori," Chania said unruffled. She wrapped herself in the cotton blanket that had thrown across the back of the couch.

Sopori's face flushed with embarrassment as he hurriedly tucked his shirt into his pants.

Khadroma looked at Chania's rumpled skirt on the floor and said, "Put it on," she instructed matter-of-factly. Khadroma carried her grocery bundles to the kitchen. There was scuffling of feet in the other room, whispers and then the quiet click of the front door closing.

"Where would you rather we go?" Chania asked as she joined her mother. She emptied one of the grocery bags and put the tea and sugar in the cabinet next to the sink. Khadroma arranged the oranges in a glass bowl.

"I told you not to bring him here."

"We didn't think you would be back so soon. You said you were out for the day."

"Don't you have any honor?" Khadroma sighed, her voice filled more with anguish than anger.

"I honor my heart. It belongs to me, not anyone else. This is a different world," Chania said. "It's not like when you and daddy were my age. The future is with the youth, with me and my friends and people like us who don't see differences, who don't care where anyone comes from or anything like that."

"Some things never change." Khadroma added, "Or they get worse. I am thinking about Uncle Rohr's wanting us to come live with him. I think maybe it's a good idea. His judgment has always been right."

"I don't know what you mean, get worse," Chania said. "I don't go to rallies. I hate politics. Not like Pandin. All my friends hate politics We're the ones who are making the new country without politics. We don't care about anybody's identity. We have good times together."

"He'll be like all the rest, Chania, mark my words."

"He's like the rest of my *friends,* if that's what you mean."

"He just wants to get into bed with you, like every boy."

"He's already done that."

"Get out," Khadroma said quietly, not turning to look at her daughter.

Chania swept a jar of sugar from the counter. White granules and sparkling glass scattered across the tiled floor, like the light snow covering the streets outside.

"I hate you," Chania said.

"No, I still don't approve. It is a very bad idea."

They had spoken on the phone several times, but this was Chania's first visit to her mother's apartment in more than a month.

The patches of snow on Chania's head that had gathered on her walk from the corner bus stop to the apartment house began to melt and trickle down her forehead. Khadroma handed her a washcloth to dry herself.

"We're getting married, with or without your approval. If you want to know, it's Sopori who insists that I invite you to the ceremony. I told him this is what you'd say. I don't expect you to understand."

"He must be a good boy, Chania," Khadroma said. "To ask for my approval. I admire him for that."

"I love him."

"I see that you love him. But there's more to think about. Love isn't everything." Khadroma took the washcloth from her daughter, folded it and put it next to the sink.

Chania stood next to her daughter.

"You're no different than all the others," Chania said. "You're prejudiced just like them. 'Don't be friends with him, marry only your own kind, don't live next to them.'" Chania mocked her mother. "Don't pretend you're not."

Khadroma asked Chania to sit down. "But first, give me some tea," she said. Chania poured steaming water into a brown mug. She dropped in a tea bag. "Sit," Khadroma said to her daughter. Khadroma stirred in three tablespoons full of sugar. She blew across the top of the cup as she gripped the handle.

Chania continued to stand.

"I want what's best for you. This isn't the best. You're still young, Chania. You don't understand people. You still think like a girl."

"And you, you think like nothing has changed. My friends aren't like what you say they are. Sopori is different. I've met his parents. They like me."

"You met his parents?"

"They have been to our apartment."

Khadroma couldn't hide her surprise. "You haven't been living with a girlfriend? I thought you were renting an apartment with one of your friends."

"I am. Sopori. He's my best friend. I never said my friend was a girl. It's what you wanted to think."

"It's OK with Sopori's parents that you living together?" Khadroma scolded.

"Yes, it's fine with them. Why wouldn't it be fine? They don't care that I'm a Bhara."

Khadroma let out a sigh of resignation. "So what do you want from me, Chania?"

"I want you to accept me," then added, "I just want you to be my mother."

Khadroma smiled fleetingly, reached for Chania but stopped before touching her daughter's elbow.

"Uncle Rohr called today."

"How is he?"

"He's worried."

"He's always worried."

"I am, too. He said that big people are saying it's time to kill all the termites." Khadroma hurried her speech. "I believe him. I think Uncle Rohr is right. It's time for us to go."

"So, you don't want me to marry Sopori?" Chania interrupted. "You go. But not me. Sopori and I are getting married. Tomorrow. He wants you to be there. And so do his parents. They said they want to meet you."

Chania glanced at her mother. She had never seen such sadness in her eyes. Suddenly she seemed much older than she remembered—the hair that was nearly gray, the liver spots on her left cheek had spread to cover most of the skin, the slump of her shoulders. She pleaded silently.

"Nothing is going to change your mind, Chania. I know that.

You've always been headstrong. Good or bad. So." She placed her hand on the small of Chania's back. "Tell me. What time is the ceremony? I'll be there. What is Sopori's family name?"

*T*he next morning it snowed again.

"Where's the fucking president?" Sopori shouted as he read the news on the Internet. Chania continued to get dressed. "Why doesn't he say something?"

There had been looting and several had been killed in ethnic neighborhoods the night before. A Bhara opposition leader had been shot dead in his home.

Sopori's question was rhetorical. He, like his friends, believed that elected officials in the government not merely condoned the violence against Bharas but were orchestrating it. Politics no longer reflected economic interests or philosophical differences, not right, left and center ideologies, but ethnic identity over all.

"Chania, we need to think about what your mother has said. Your Uncle Rohr . . ."

"Why would anyone bother us?" she interjected. "Not when we're married. Who cares about politics anyhow?"

"Maybe they won't bother me. But I don't know. Because you will be my wife, that's makes me a traitor in some eyes. Look at me, Chania," Sopori said, putting his hands on her shoulders and looking into her eyes. "I'm not enough to protect you."

"Can we talk about this later, Sopori?" Chania fastened the clasp of a beaded necklace, admired herself in the mirror and brushed her hair. "I don't want to spoil our wedding day. And don't talk to my mother about this, either. Promise me."

"Yes, I promise, Chania. Not until after the wedding. I won't.

But promise *me,* Chania," Sopori said, more sternly than Chania had heard him before. "After the wedding you will listen to me."

"What?"

Sopori's comment startled Chania. She looked at him and for a fleeting moment thought of canceling the wedding.

"Let's go," he said. "Your mother is waiting for us to collect her."

"We have until noon for the license. Any time before that is OK. Don't rush me."

"We told your mother we would get her at 10. With the snow it will take us a half hour to get there. It's already past ten."

"She can wait."

When the digital numbers on the clock changed to "3" and "0," Chania was ready. They drove across town in Sopori's Toyota sedan. The snow kept most people indoors but every few blocks men and boys, many wearing balaclavas, were moving in drifts, the horde opening and closing like flocks of domesticated pigeons released daily from rooftop coops throughout the city.

Early winter presented additional hazards on the road. Sopori drove slowly, aware of the black ice under the pure snow. Approaching each intersection, he braked lightly, tapping the pedal until the car came to a gentle stop.

Since leaving the house, he and Chania hadn't exchanged a word. The only sound was the crunch of snow under the tires.

"Call your mother," Sopori said. "Tell her were almost there."

Chania punched the numbers on her cell phone. No answer.

"She's probably waiting for us downstairs."

"Well, we are late," Sopori said sharply.

When they arrived, Sopori parked the car at the end of the street.

"I don't see her. What's her cell number?" he asked.

"She doesn't have a cell phone," Chania said.

"I'll run up to get her." Sopori began to open the door.

"No, I'll do it," Chania said.

She stepped onto the street, glad to feel the brace of cold air on her face. She took small steps to keep herself from sliding. She balanced herself against the apartment house wall. Her hand brushed against a poster plastered on the brick.

Despite the cold, the glass door to the apartment house was open. Pasted across the front door:

Frozen slush covered the vestibule floor. As Chania hurriedly walked up two flights of steps to her mother's flat, she slipped on a puddle of melting snow on the marble staircase and grasped the iron railing before tripping.

The door to her mother's apartment was open. Chania called her mother. No one answered. A chair in the living room was tipped on its side. Chania went into her mother's bedroom. Bed blankets were strewn on the floor.

Chania turned and dashed down the stairs. She noticed that the apartment doors on each landing were ajar. Aside from the rapid clack of her boot heels on the steps, there was only silence as she rushed outside.

Chania waved to Sopori to meet her. He drove the car the wrong way down the one-way street.

"She's gone!" Chania said as she climbed into the passenger seat. "Everyone's gone!"

"What?"

"There's no one in the building. It's empty. I have to find her. It's my fault. It's my fault. I shouldn't have made her wait."

Tracks made by many feet led from the apartment house entrance down the street and around the corner. Sopori and Chania followed them in the car for several blocks, until the road was choked with people and they couldn't pass.

Above the heads in the crowd a ten-foot tall, inflated termite rocked in the wind.

"They're going towards the drainage canal."

Chania fumbled to open the car door.

"What are you doing, Chania?"

"I've got to find my mother. She's in the crowd. I can see one of our neighbors. I know she's here."

"Don't be foolish. This is too dangerous for you. Stay here."

"Everyone's being taken away. I have to get her. I should have gotten her when I said I would."

"Stop it, Chania. What do you think you can do? You can't stop them. They'll take you, too."

Chania ignored Sopori. She ran from the car, threw off her high heel boots and ran after the throng as they smashed the gate to the canal. Chania was swallowed by the mob as it rushed down the embankment.

Sopori jumped out of the car, turned his ankle as he stepped down onto the ice and grabbed the door before falling. He tried to run but his ankle buckled under him and he fell to the ice, his head hitting the sidewalk. Blood seeped into his eye. In a blur, he watched the mob flow down the embankment, the rubber termite the last thing to disappear from view. Sopori took his cell phone from his parka and called the police. He re-dialed after a dozen unanswered rings.

Now a busy signal. Again. Again.

In the distance, sirens.

(E)RUCTION (D)ISORDER

*B*EING RICH MEANT HAVING A HOME BY THE LAKE, a fishing boat big enough for friends and a trip to Manhattan every once in a while. It wasn't that Durrell didn't know what real wealth was; he saw plenty of it around him, especially in the summer. Rather, he couldn't imagine having that kind of money for himself.

For most of his time growing up in Saratoga Springs, Durrell was surrounded by deteriorated and neglected buildings in a city that seemed destined for a lingering death. In recent years, the town made a dramatic recovery. Now when Durrell walked by many of the Victorian mansions (more than a thousand, one brochure from the Chamber of Commerce claims) that still line the streets, houses built by the very rich to be near the mineral waters that spout from the earth throughout the area, he saw that many had been rehabilitated. Most of the fine houses, displaying their former glory, have been converted to offices or sub-divided into apartments, but it wasn't hard to imagine what life was like a

119

century ago. The elegant baths and hotels that the rich frequented are largely gone but for one. Still, in the last several years, Durrell could see wealth first-hand as tourists arrive during the summer, a few nearly as rich as their predecessors. They come to watch the thoroughbreds, some of which they own, for a week or two at the historic racetrack.

One day while Durrell was rewiring an old mansion recently bought by what his friend told him was "a financial engineer and entrepreneur," to be used by the owner only during racing season, a transport trailer pulled up in the circular driveway. Unlike a horse transport vehicle with slatted sides, the trailer was enclosed, without windows or ventilation. Durrell watched as the back door of the trailer opened. The roar of a powerful engine echoed and after a quarter hour a metallic orange car with doors that flipped up like wings of a diving seabird (Durrell had never seen any car like this before) was slowly driven down the plank.

The driver, Durrell learned, wasn't the owner but the car's handler—its groom, caretaker, mechanic, minder, bodyguard and babysitter. He drove the trailer for the owner from one of his homes to another: Miami, Amagansett and Saratoga Springs. The cars were otherwise kept in a sky garage in a condo in Manhattan.

"What *is* it?" Durrell wondered.

Durrell, whose interest in cars amounted to reading automotive magazines in the barbershop, knew the make but not the model but kept his ignorance to himself.

The handler walked back into the transporter. An engine roared and ten minutes later another car descended—cobalt blue with duel vents on the roof, red fenders and doors, and an exposed motor behind the driver's seat.

Durrell asked the wrangler about the car. Durrell never heard of this make and forgot its name before the end of the day. But he remembered well what he saw—the two most expensive cars in the world. It was better than watching a mare give birth.

Durrell had often thought of owning a sports car: a Mustang or Camaro or, in his dreams, a Nissan 370Z. To think that he could own a million dollar car was like believing that because he played miniature golf he could win the U.S. Open. With luck, if he stumbled into a good paying job or inherited some cash or won the lottery or put his money on the right horse, he could at least live, if not an easy life, a pleasurable one.

Not until he bought his own house in foreclosure, a sad clapboard cabin with a sagging porch and leaking windows, did Durrell find that he had stumbled upon a money pot that was literally under his feet. It was the mineral water, the same that thousands used when they came to "take the baths" at the Gideon Putnam Hotel, soaking in dirt brown bubbly water at $20 a half hour, hoping to cure injuries, skin ailments and arthritis, the same that visitors drank at the ever-running fountains where they can take as much as they want from the underground springs—Big Red, Charlie, Old Iron, Polaris, High Rock or any of the other dozen scattered throughout the city.

Neither Durrell nor his friends bothered with the mineral water. Like most residents, they ignored the peculiar tasting waters. Appreciating its restorative properties was left to a handful of Native Americans who lived a few miles out of town and people like Durrell's grandparents. They paid no heed to what they ate, but they wouldn't go a meal without a glass of mineral water and one more before going to sleep. Every few weeks they drove into town with large plastic bottles to collect water from four different springs.

"This one is for digestion," Pops explained to Durrell years ago. "Take it when your plumbing isn't working good."

"Why do you and Grandma drink it every morning?" Durrell asked.

"When you're old, you need to make sure things stay in working order. Preventative maintenance."

The afternoon drink was for pains in the joints, that with dinner for the skin. His grandmother said the water she drank before going to bed was better than a sleeping pill. It put the mind at ease knowing that what you got for free from a tap downtown was better for you than pills made in a factory.

"There are waters for everything," Durrell was told many times. His grandparents gave him a sheet from the Lincoln Mineral Spring: "Physicians believe that Mineral Springs facilitate healing in many ways such as increasing blood circulation and cell oxygenation; increasing body metabolism; promoting feelings of physical and psychological well-being; helping with psoriasis and fungal infections; stimulating the immune system; and normalizing gland function and the autonomic nervous system."

"Is there anything that it isn't good for?" he asked his grandmother. She looked at her husband.

"Yeah, but you don't want to know. You're too young."

Durrell had to take their word for the cures they claimed. He couldn't stand the taste of what they drank. Water from one spring seemed worse than the other. He always left their house thirsty. Fortunately for him, Durrell's parents dismissed the talk of mineral water cures as hokum and didn't keep any in the house when he was young. They'll stick with the bottled water they get in the convenience store, thank you, a practice Durrell followed now that he was an adult himself.

*H*aving enough savings from his job as an electrician at the raceway and from moonlighting on non-union work he did around town, Durrell was able to buy the materials to replace his porch and build a new one, paint three rooms that had never been painted before, and purchase a couch and 3D TV. When he finished caulking the windows, he began construction of a new room on the back of the house, a project he had to abandon when he cracked a rock that began to seep water.

"Damn it," he said. He didn't know that the house sat on the edge of a bog. The foundation would be too unstable to support the extension.

His grandparents didn't share Durrell's disappointment.

"This is mineral water," his grandfather said as he scooped the water into his palm. He touched it with his tongue.

"The temperature's right, about 50 degrees." Because it had little odor, Durrell was skeptical.

"Are you sure?" His grandmother rolled some around in her mouth. "Certain," she said. "Not much carbonation."

His grandfather peered at the mud.

"There're bubbles here. Small. That's the carbonation. All the waters have some carbonation. Some more than others."

"It's really salty, though," his grandmother said, cupping her hand for another drink. "More than Hathorn #3."

His grandfather said it was too salty to drink.

"Maybe," his grandmother said, as she filled empty Poland

Spring Water bottles Durrell had scattered behind the house. "But it might be good for something."

Aside from the seventeen public springs around town, a few other minor springs had been uncovered around the city on private property. None produced sufficient amounts or that of a distinctive quality to make it noteworthy.

The next time Durrell saw his grandparents, his grandfather told him that he had gone to check the location of Durrell's house on geologic map in the library.

"We were right, Durrell," he said.

The house, it turned out, was built just slightly to the east of the Saratoga fault that runs from Whitehall to Albany. A line could be drawn from several springs straight to Durrell's house. Laying the foundation for the extension had created a small fissure in the shale just below the thin layer of soil, allowing water that was deep in the earth to percolate through the dolostone into Durrell's backyard.

This was the first new spring to be found in Saratoga in nearly a century.

"It's mineral water. No doubt."

"We've been drinking it. We like it."

His grandmother had come prepared; she poured glassfuls of water into a five-gallon bucket. She snapped the lid shut and his grandfather put it into the trunk of his car. When they returned to Durrell's house ten days later, they filled two dozen two liter used plastic soda bottles. His grandmother said that they had given some of Durrell's mineral water to their friends at the senior center.

"Everyone likes it," his grandfather said. "You know Maryanne?

"LaBeouf?"

"Yes. She's crazy about it."

"They're all asking for us to bring some. They've all given us bottles to fill for them."

What was so special about this water? Durrell wanted to know. This was the only spring water that prevented an embarrassing ailment of many old people, they said.

His grandfather joked, "You know, old people suffer from ED." He waited to see the expression on his grandson's face. "Not just men, either."

His grandmother laughed.

"Eruction disorder," his grandfather explained with a smile. "That's what we call it."

"You don't belch," his grandmother said with a small smile on her face. "Other spring waters make you bloated. This one does the opposite. It stops you from feeling full and belching. It makes the gas go away. It's embarrassing, belching in public. We try to make jokes about it, but mostly we just pretend like nothing's happened."

"It also stops farting," his grandfather added. "It's good for problems at both ends. E.D. It's great. It's like the clubhouse air has been scrubbed clean. It's a preventative air freshener."

"The water calms the nerves in the stomach. It's an antacid. Low in carbonation."

They went on about the virtues of Durrell's water as they returned each week to refill their bottles.

*T*he proposition was this: Durrell's grandparents would pay to dig a well in his backyard and bottle the spring water themselves, then sell the 12 oz. bottled water for $1 a piece and Durrell would receive half the profits. Durrell thought that the idea wouldn't work. There was plenty of spring water around town, all of it for free. Locally bottled water was never a big seller. Stores and vending machines were stocked with big name brands. But he had nothing to lose. His grandparents were going to do all the work. They would get testimonials from their friends—who swear that drinking a glass a day made the air in the clubroom as fresh as outdoors—print labels, make fliers and hawk their product down the Thruway as far as Syracuse and Rochester and up the Northway to Lake George and beyond.

Since it didn't require any outlay on his part, Durrell accepted their offer. Once the operation began, on Saturdays he pasted labels onto bottles and loaded crates full of mineral water into his grandparent's camper van. His grandparents talked to managers in convenience stores and coffee shops; they convinced owners of a few B&Bs to offer them to guests. But it was mostly word-of-mouth (an appropriate expression for the product, his grandfather said), spreading from one senior citizen to another, that sold (E) (D)'s Sparkling Health Water. Senior Centers within a hundred mile radius of Saratoga Springs began to stock the water; there were orders from retirement homes and assisted living facilities. They had to get a telephone number just for the company. And Al LaBeouf, Maryanne's son, created a website for the mineral water. They copyrighted the name.

In less than a year, they sold enough mineral water to buy a new and larger van and to pay the salary of a part-time deliveryman—a woman, actually, Maryanne LaBeouf who brought bottles to the senior centers around Saratoga. There was no better advertisement than her enthusiasm for the water. She would open a bottle and sit with players at a card table or hand a glass to men playing pool. She gave away samples in small bottles.

Before the year's end there was a small profit, an accomplishment that came as a surprise to Durrell. At first he had indulged his grandparents but now, for the first time in years, he didn't need to work overtime or find after-hours jobs. Profits increased again when a soda and beer distributor took on their mineral water.

*A*mused by the success of his unlikely product, Durrell used his cell phone to make a video that he downloaded to YouTube.

He stood with a bottle in his hand and his grandparents in the background.

(Rude noises caused by air released through the pinched neck of a balloon.)

It can happen any time. You have to be ready. Did you know that E.D. affects an estimated tens of millions of men and women in the United States alone?

(Durrell's grandparents sit sadly around a small table.)

Eruction Disorder. You are not alone. A bummer for you and the ones you love.

(His grandmother belches.)

You don't have to be ashamed of your ED (His grandfather hangs his head.)

Are you embarrassed to be around friends?

(A loud sound. His grandfather looks around and shrugs his shoulders, disclaiming responsibility.)

Do people want to run the other way when they see you coming?

(Another long, rude sound. His grandmother fans her hand in front of her face. She coughs. His grandfather looks sheepish.)

Search no longer for an E.D. cure. Get big relief the natural way. Safe, guaranteed treatment.

(He holds up a bottle of (E)(D)'s, untwists the cap and pours a drink.)

(E)(D)'s Sparkling Health Water sweetens your breath, soothes your stomach and freshens the air.

(His grandparents are laughing.) And it's good for you.

(An explosive fart. Durrell's grandparents look at one another, walk to a man leaning on a cane and offer him a drink.)

Be a Good Samaritan. Drink (E)(D)'s Sparkling Health Water every day. It's natural. It's good for you and for the environment. Salud!

(His grandparents and the man with the cane drain their glasses. Everyone laughs.)

The video went viral—10,000 hits the first day, 30,000 by the end of the week and the next week more than a half million. A story about the video appeared in The Saratogian and was nationally syndicated. Durrell and his grandparents didn't know how to cope with the phone calls from around the country.

But there was even a bigger shock for Durrell: his grandparents were quitting.

"No more for us," his grandfather said. "This stuff isn't good."

Durrell didn't know what to say.

"Two people in our center had strokes last week."

"So?"

"And last month, three more."

"Since they started drinking the water, it's been like an epidemic."

"I've stopped."

"Me, too."

"Come on. How do you know it's the water?" Durrell asked. "It could be a coincidence."

"From all over I'm hearing the same thing. It's no good."

"The salt," his grandmother said. "It raises the blood pressure. It's causing strokes, Durrell. There's no question about it."

"Since when are you doctors?"

Now it was their turn to be speechless. He had never talked to them like that.

"I'm sorry, but just because some people are getting strokes doesn't mean that it's the water that's doing it. Lots of people get strokes, lots of old people. It's what old people do."

"I'll tell you," his grandfather said, his lips trembling as he tried to suppress his anger. "Everyone who drinks the water has high blood pressure." He stopped for a moment to calm down. "You know, we take our pressure regularly at the center. A nurse comes by every month. And we have a machine at home. We use it every night. The nurse says she'd never seen anything like it. Everyone—everyone—has high blood pressure. Even those who didn't have it before."

"It's killing us," Durrell's grandmother said.

"I stopped and now my pressure's back to normal."

*S*oon after his grandparents quit, leaving the business to him, Durrell received a letter, followed by a phone call, from a natural and organic food company wanting to acquire (E)(D)'s Sparkling

Health Water to add to their list of soy milk, seasonings, grains, snacks, juice, pet food, teas, and skin care products. Heaven & Earth proposed a deal and sent a contract. After checking with a lawyer and finding no obvious flaws, Durrell, over his grandparents' objections, accepted. The offer was too good to turn down. With prudent investments, his lawyer assured him, he would never have to work again.

Durrell's idea of prudence and that of the lawyer's were miles (furlongs) apart. He didn't want to settle for a modest life in upstate New York. So Durrell placed the biggest bet of his life. He took all the money from the buyout and bought the major share in a thoroughbred filly from a stable in Texas, a horse with a modest pedigree. Once again, Durrell was luckier than he could have imagined. As soon as At Your Own Risk was old enough, she was entered into Grade I Stakes and went to an undefeated 16 races before being retired to become a successful broodmare, producing nine foals.

From this fortune, Durrell bought himself two cars and a transporter. He traveled from Saratoga to Gulfstream, Del Mar and Churchill Downs, Belmont and back home again, happy to live in the two-bedroom house left to him by his grandparents when they died.

CORAL FISH

*I*T'S NOT THAT ANYTHING'S WRONG WITH MY DNA. All the tests come back clean. This means that my problem isn't genetic and that my only hope is to change my feelings. I desperately want to, but no matter how hard I try, I can't. I've locked myself away for months thinking about my transgression and I've talked to counselors and friends, but while I know I shouldn't be this way, deep down I feel that most people would think the same thing. It would be much better if I was contrite, but I'm not. I can't *make* myself feel sorry. But as long as I feel the way I do, I will have to live with being shunned. I will live in internal exile.

You won't understand my condition and my sister's death if you don't live here, since this is one of the few communities to make my offense a crime. So I better explain the background since I don't know you or where you are from and my dilemma won't make sense unless I present the big picture.

*S*everal generations ago things had gotten so bad with all kinds of dishonesty and greed and violence that the world reached a critical point. Many human-made disasters plagued us. We didn't have breathable air or drinkable water and our food was poisoning us, mostly because we didn't know how to control our appetites. We felt entitled to everything; if we could dream it, we consumed it. There were also constant terrorist attacks, wars between countries, civil wars, ethnic cleansings and gang wars. Looking back, it's pretty clear that this was a kind of collective suicide, with no one able to put a stop to it. It was the part of human nature, the bad part that was ruling and ruining everything. Cumulatively making the world unlivable.

Then one day the world changed. It was literally overnight. Many believers, Christians and Muslims, attributed this to the Second Coming of Jesus or the Mahdi, while for Jews it was the Messiah coming for the first time or, if not the actual arrival of the Messiah, then clearly some sort of divine intervention was at play. In India and other parts of South Asia, it was a sign that the Age of Iron had run its course and a new Age of Gold had arrived tens of thousands of years earlier than predicated by holy books and their interpreters. Those given to conspiracies said that aliens had secretly landed and did something to our minds. One explanation seemed as plausible as any other. Something miraculous had happened, something that brought about heaven on earth or utopia, take your pick.

Most now believe that this historic change occurred naturally. Initially, this seemed a preposterous theory, but now it is as accepted as the theory of evolution itself. The insight regarding the change came from marine biologists, who observed spontaneous sex changes in fish. Once thought relatively rare, found only amongst a handful of species of coral fish, the conversion from one sex to the other turns out to be fairly common. The mechanisms of this phenomenon in fish are well known and it seems likely that something very similar had occurred with human beings. We still don't know precisely why this happened with humans, but it apparently had to do with evolutionary survival. The human race had been headed for extinction and the change increased the odds for survival—or something like that. Other scientists say that the timing was pure luck. The change happened spontaneously, the way every million years or so the magnetic poles switch places just like that.

I don't really understand much about science myself. But here is how the conventional wisdom goes today: The fear that humanity felt before The Great Dawn was so great that it caused a change in people's genetic chain. Humans shed their devilish, self-centered instincts so as to allow the angelic altruistic side to emerge.

Neurobiologists say that as a result of enough genes mutating this way that our behavior, which used to resemble a chimp's, is now is more like that of a happy-go-lucky bonobo. Bonobos look like chimps but prefer romping in the bushes to beating each other on the head. The pleasure center of our brains now responds to cooperation and harmony, just it once did to money, sugar, power, and drugs. Our instinct for self-preservation turned out to be stronger than our urge for self-gratification. So we mutated, all of us, just like that.

I know that before the Great Dawn people used to say that "now everything is different" after a big war or when a technological innovation was introduced. But this was really true after the genetic change. Human nature was upside down and inside out from what it had been just the day before and, everyone agreed, the world was far better than ever in human history.

One of the great surprises right after the Great Dawn was that, despite the predictions of people who like to forecast the future, religion and politics didn't wither away. Rather they have flourished. I think there are more types of government than there has ever been. There are direct democracies and representative forms of government; there are places where the majority counts, other places that use weighted counts and every other way of vote counting and figuring out fair and just representation. There are areas where elders make the important decisions and other regions where children are included from the earliest age.

Something that also might seem odd to you is that there are no passports or visas needed to go from one community to another. There are borders but they are completely open. People are free to come and go as they please. A few move many times to find the right fit for themselves, but most of us like what we have and where we were born. Mostly we stay put because we are convinced our way of doing things is the best. We aren't all happy or always happy, but nearly everyone is and those who aren't aren't discontent either.

As for religion: Taking the human makeover as a sign from God or the gods or bodhisattvas or whatever, worship services have soared. The Great Dawn won over many agnostics and even some atheists, as it was living proof of that religion was no myth or wishful thinking. The prayers aren't any longer prayers of petition but ones of praise and gratitude and from this have followed music and art on a level that the world hadn't seen for more than a millennium. Religion has been drained of fear and submission. Throughout the world religion is either joy or sober contemplation or ecstatic experiences, depending upon personal temperament.

I've tried different religions, too, as part of my wanting to change and hoping I can rid myself of this curse, but that path, like everything else I've tried, comes to nothing.

I'm guilty as charged—I admit that—and I should be punished. Everyone needs to accept the judgment of the law. I'm not exempt from it and I don't think I should be. After all, our laws were arrived democratically by people of good will and they are applied fairly. Even now I am free to leave. It's my choice. There are communities that would take me since they don't have the same laws that we do and what I feel isn't a crime according to them. But I don't want to go. I would be separated from everything I love and I can't think of any punishment worse than forced emigration. Being ostracized is almost as intolerable but not quite.

What I have begun to think is that maybe my community's approach to this is wrong after all. When communities were first established, The Founders argued about whether society should be concerned only with what people do or whether their character, intentions and feelings should also be judged. Most communities decided that all that could and ought to be criminalized are actions. What you did was all that mattered. Think what you like, but you can't hurt others. But The Founders of my community decided otherwise. In their wisdom, they concluded that behavior and intentions are of one piece. What's more, they said that what was in your heart was the equivalent of taking an action. People are good only if their intentions are virtuous and their hearts are pure. And you are a bad person if your intentions or feelings and thoughts are bad, even if you don't act on them. Therefore, our constitution lists varying degrees of epicaricacy as a crime. Mine is first-degree.

There are two analogies in *The Founders' Papers,* which are read by every high school student, that clinched the debate. The first one said, suppose there are two people who are identical in wealth and expenses. One day they are walking down the street when they see a beggar. The first person stops and is brought to tears by the beggar's tale of woe, and out of the goodness of her heart, tenderly places $5 in his hand. Shortly after, the second person walks by. He doesn't cry at the sight of the poor man, as did the first passer-by. He is in a rush to get on with his own business, but because his religion demands that he give 10% of his income to the poor, he drops $100 into the beggar's cup. Now, we can see that the first person did the better thing because she gave from her heart while the second person gave because it was an obligation. The first was the good person, the second only following rules.

If that was all, then my offense would be strictly a moral failure, as it is elsewhere, not a crime. But the second argument came from the Christian bible. It is quoted in *The Founders' Papers:* "You have heard that it was said, Do not commit adultery. But I tell you that anyone who looks at a woman lustfully has already committed adultery with her in his heart." They also quoted this verse: "Anyone who hates a brother or sister is a murderer, and you know very well that eternal life and murder don't go together." The Founders took this to mean that we have to be pure in our hearts and that our feelings count at least as much as our actions. The example turned out to be hypothetical since adultery, like many other vanished vices, doesn't happen. No one lusts after someone who is married to another person or lusts after anyone but his or her own spouse. But there have been rare instances of being guilty of coveting another's possessions. Rarer still, but no unheard of, is wanting to hurt someone.

A little gene therapy combined with solitude lead to penitence (the original idea for what you may have called a 'penitentiary') has always worked.

But it hasn't worked this time, not for me. My crime is one step less than murder but it involves an innocent child, so it is very serious. Here is the situation: When I first learned about my mother's misfortune early in her marriage, I was saddened. I felt sorry for what my parents must have felt, losing a child like that, days after giving birth. They keep the only photo they have of the infant in an envelope in their dresser drawer. I asked my mother who this was when I first saw it. My mother's eyes moistened and it took her several minutes before she could compose herself long enough to explain that Linda was less than a month old when she died, without warning, in her crib one night. She hadn't been sick or anything. They never found out why she died. This was hard for my mother to say to me and I was upset that I had asked her. Now I wish I never knew.

When I thought about it, it occurred to me that if my infant sister hadn't died, I probably would never have been born and I am glad that I was. I'm here because she isn't. I have figured out that I am the replacement child. So I am pleased that my baby sister died. I can't rid myself of that feeling. The truth is if she hadn't, I wouldn't have been conceived since my parents have often said that they never wanted more than one child. So my sister died and I'm not sorry that she did. In fact, I'm glad and that's what makes me such a bad person, feeling thankful for the misfortune of three people.

I like my life—or at least I did until I found out the condition under which I was born—and I can't stop feeling the way I do. If I wasn't glad about Linda's death, then I wouldn't think my own life was worth living. Because if I wasn't glad about her death, it would be the same as wishing that I had never been born. And if I wished that, I would find myself in the same predicament since I would be guilty of not wanting to live, which is the same thing as thinking about suicide. Such violent thoughts are also punishable.

$\mathcal{T}$hese ruminations have convinced me that it is best for me to leave everything I love and join another community, where feelings and thoughts aren't treated the same as actions, where epicaricacy isn't a crime.

But—

I know I won't be happy there; a loveless life is no life at all. And I can't stand the thought of being separated from my parents and my friends. I know I wouldn't be happy in a community where people believe that the heartless person who does good things because he is supposed to is just as good as the generous person who is good for its own sake.

Happiness anywhere else is impossible for me, so how can life be worthwhile? If I didn't care what it would do to my loved ones, I would kill myself. That would hurt my parents beyond repair. They are happy that I was born. Why can't I be?

IN TREASURED TEAPOTS

GREG KIRIMA PLANNED TO BREAK THE TEAPOTS one pot at a time, as his homage to Clifford Rao, an idea that came to him when he unexpectedly inherited the collection soon after the poet's death.

It was Rao's influence that led Greg to his own career as a writer. The poet had exposed Greg to a way of life that he had never dreamed of as a child. Greg's upbringing was unexceptional—never boring or challenging, simply ordinary. He supposed that's why he wrote about the lives of others and hardly mentioned himself. His own life would never make for a best-selling memoir. Greg childhood was devoid of divorce, abuse, drunkenness, addiction or poverty. His parents fulfilled their duties by providing him with a comfortable home, making sure he went to school with clean clothes and by putting food that he enjoyed on the table three times a day. He never asked for more of anything or questioned whether his parents loved him because he didn't know there was more to ask for and even if he did, Greg didn't think he would have wanted it. As far as he was concerned, a good childhood is one where parents leave you alone, where adults have their lives and children theirs. Greg was content as a child and as happy as anyone was entitled to be.

Greg was satisfied in that life—until he discovered Rao. It was as though windows were thrown open and for the first time he realized that he had been breathing re-cycled and stale air.

Greg heard about Rao in his sophomore year in college. He read Rao's poems, in an anthology of American poets, the poems taking up two pages of small print. To this day, Rao's poems are standard in European textbooks and he is considered one of the greatest poets of the mid-20th century, but in America he has fallen out of the pantheon of noted artists, his books are out of print and there's not even a scornful reference to him in a contemporary poetry anthology.

*D*iane, a fellow student he met in a bookstore on Columbus Avenue, invited Greg to a happening in a studio loft not far from their college and it was as though the world had broken apart to reveal countless vistas. At the gatherings there were no rules, no restrictions, random couplings and un-couplings, a cornucopia of new sensations and thoughts. Rao was one of the regulars. Greg remembers Rao opened a dictionary, closed his eyes and ran his finger down the page. He then read the word and asked someone for the first word that popped into his mind. Next he called for a page and line number, returned to the dictionary to select another word, continuing this process until a timer rang, stopping the creation; he then read the collected words in reverse order, all the while jumping on a trampoline. Another time he stood silently for the entire night in front of a lectern. Greg remembers another happening where Rao cut up works of other poets, then randomly strung together the fragments and chose the title for the poem the address of the loft. One poem was the letter 'I' repeated a hundred times, interspersed with five letter 'U's. He entitled it "Modern Times." It was during this period that in an interview in *Playboy* magazine, he answered every question by simply echoing the interviewer.

Rao had become a celebrity, appearing in concerts reading his work, joking and pontificating with Steve Allen and David Frost, debating politicians with cutting wit, signing petitions, being honored by cultural institutions, a part of a coterie of painters and avant-garde musicians who appeared on the cover of *Time* magazine in a group photo. He demonstrated for nuclear disarmament and disrupted traffic on bridges and tunnels with faux funerals to protest the war in Vietnam. Rao often used tongue-in-cheek irony in interviews, while other times blistering social criticism was the weapon of choice.

As brightly as his star lit the sky of America, it was eclipsed by new criticism and changing tastes. First, the public tired of Rao's aleatory antics and his sententious pronouncements. When his poems took a traditional and romantic turn, he lost all favor. Poetry, he said without irony, was the language of love in all its anguish. Poems are songs of the beating heart of the universe seeking salvation through love. Words were the salve for the wounds that the love brings, all sentiments that consigned him to high culture's netherworld.

An article about Rao in an influential literary journal derided his poetry as bathetic. And with that confluence he was made doubly invisible: by the indifference of the public and the ridicule of the critics. His colleagues moved headlong into the future while Rao turned his back to all that and walked over the horizon.

He moved to France and while his poems were lauded there, he refused to appear in public and rejected all requests for interviews. This only added to his irrelevance for some and to his mystique for others.

*W*hen Greg graduated from college, he bought a used Fiat with money that he had inherited from an uncle and started a cross-country trip, reaching the four corners of the continental US. Diane started out with him but they split up in northern Maine where she complained about the cold, the same complaint Greg had but not about the weather. The next month he met a married woman in Ohio who had recently separated from her husband and they traveled together as far as Idaho. There she declared that she missed her husband and took a Trailways bus back East. Greg traveled with three more female companions before returning to New York a year and a half later.

The people and towns along the borders of Canada and Mexico intrigued Greg. He wrote articles for several magazines, and then published a book based on the pieces. Following the same theme, his next book, *Borders,* took him to Europe where he wrote about Northern Ireland and the "Troubles" in Strabane; the Free University in Brussels that was divided into autonomous Flemish and Walloon administrations that refused to acknowledge one another's existence; East and West Berlin; the tiny villages of Crassier and Crassy on the French-Swiss border; and the island called Saint Martin on one side and St. Marteen on the other.

Borders was favorably reviewed on the front page of the *Times Literary Supplement* and remained on the New York *Times* bestseller list for a year. His next book was on fusion cuisine, followed by one on syncretistic religions and another on code-switching languages, highlighting Spanglish and Llanito. His biggest seller focused on the lives of secret cross-dressers. For the last half-dozen years, Greg edited a weekly culture magazine and often was a guest on the Charlie Rose show.

Rao's writings and his performances now seemed jejune to Greg. But he appreciated them for what they were: part of an era when everything was questioned, every authority needing to defend its privileges, all boundaries to be crossed. It was a time when life was freed by the imagination linked to courage.

Greg received an email from the woman he had scarcely thought about since his road trip but he remembered her in some detail. She hoped that this was the right Gregory Kirima, Diane wrote, the one she had once dated, the one whose books she admired for years and whose column she regularly read. She couldn't tell from the images of him on the Internet but she thought that he probably was the right one.

She often thought about getting in touch with him, she said, but life has a way of getting in the way. After she left Maine she married a law student, "but I divorced as soon as my husband made partner in a big time firm in New York. I had helped him so much with his studies I thought I knew as much about the law as he did. I was right. Law school was a breeze." Diane concluded her email by asking Greg if it would be all right for her to phone him.

As soon as he finished reading the email, Greg wrote back. He didn't know why he responded so quickly. He gave her his phone number and encouraged her to call him "at any time." Maybe he had read her wrong when he was young, that restlessness and longing, not her, had been the problem and that, as he thought about it, he probably would have left him, too.

He found a message on his voice mail the next day and he returned the call before taking off his sweatshirt.

"Do you remember Clifford Rao?" Diane asked, getting to the point of her call quickly. Greg, settling in, felt disappointment. "The poet."

"Of course I remember." He struggled with his jacket as he held the phone in one hand. "Hold on a second." He put the phone down on the desk, pulled off his hoodie and dropped it on the floor beside the chair. "OK. Rao? Sure I remember. Why? How could I forget?"

"He died last week," she said.

"Really? I didn't know he was still alive." Greg couldn't hide his irritation. He expected something different than her businesslike approach. Well, Maine, he thought. "Where did you hear that? I didn't see his obit."

"There was a notice in the *Times* last Wednesday."

"You know, I haven't thought about him in years. I thought he died years ago, you know. So, you saw an obit? I don't read the death notices."

Diane said, "Neither do I. But I was the one who put this one in."

"You? Why you?" Greg walked to the refrigerator and pulled the door open with his free hand.

"I am the executor of the estate. Listen. I can explain it to you in person. It's a little complicated."

Greg remained silent. He took out a Styrofoam container with half of last night's dinner from The Fatted Goose.

"Listen," she said. "I'm going to start putting his things in order. I thought you could meet me there. I thought you'd be interested."

"There? Where's there?"

"Rao lived in Prospect Heights."

"Brooklyn? Are you serious? Brooklyn? Really? He's lived here in the city all these years? I thought he was in France."

"Yes. Well, when his wife died," Diane said, "Clifford moved from France back to New York. But he didn't want to see anyone from his old life. In fact, he seldom left his apartment at all. I was about the only person he had contact with."

A pang of regret rose in Greg. He hadn't wanted to leave that part of his past behind so thoroughly. If he had only known he was so close by, he would have at least met with him to tell him how important he had been to him.

"I wished I had known. I would loved to have seen him."

"He wouldn't have agreed to see you or even to have talked to you on the phone." Why was he feeling competitive with this woman he hadn't seen in many years? "He didn't respond to anyone. Not even his family. He was completely private. He and Livia were practically recluses."

She was inviting Greg to the Raos' apartment because she thought he might want to write an article about Rao. It was only right that he be recognized, at least for what he once was and what he meant.

"Well, do you want to meet me tomorrow?"

"Of course I do. Of course," he said eagerly to his own surprise.

Greg took out his laptop and while waiting for his food to be heated in the microwave read the death notice in the Times. Further searches led him to several long and laudatory obituaries in French. Wikipedia's entry about Clifford Rao was ten sentences long, an entry that Greg had never thought of searching for.

*T*he Beaux Arts apartment building, stood across from the park, off the crazy spiral of streets by Grand Army Plaza. The marble floor gleamed and a large vase filled with sunflowers towered in the center of the lobby. The doorman, seated behind a high podium, phoned the apartment to announce him.

"The elevator to the left," the doorman said. "Fourth floor."

Greg pulled the scissor gate closed and the elevator rose slowly in a rumble. How European, he thought.

A woman in a black fitted skirt, high heels and silk blouse opened the apartment. Her hair now hugged her head like a white karakul hat. From her neck hung a double-strand necklace. Expensive gems, Greg knew, but had no idea which. No matter how he tried to fit what he saw with what he remembered, this was scarcely the shambling girl who set out cross-country with him.

"Gregory."

He stood.

"Nice to see you again. Thanks for coming," she said. "You look fit."

What the hell does that mean? How should you greet an old boyfriend—no, friend—, one not seen in forty years? He stood awkwardly, his hands shoved in the pockets of his jacket, thinking that it would have been better if he hadn't worn his canvas sneakers.

"Come in," Diane said, lightly touching his sleeve and pulling him slightly towards her. She kissed him on the cheek. "Welcome to Rao's digs. Can I get you a drink? There are a few things in the liquor cabinet."

They sat on a wide window ledge overlooking traffic circling the Soldiers' and Sailors' triumphal arch. No wonder he took this apartment, Greg thought. So much like Paris. Greg wondered if the main branch of the library just a couple of blocks away had any of Rao's books.

The apartment was spare: the walls without pictures or paintings, no rugs on the floors, no ornaments, knickknacks or mementos on shelves or sideboards, the items that made a place more than a shelter. Except for a dozen photos of Clifford and Livia—the two of them smiling and embracing, all taken indoors—that filled a small end table.

Diane told Greg that when she left him on their road trip and returned to New York, she continued to attend Rao's performances and eventually became a groupie in the coterie of artists that put on the happenings.

"You know, when he met Livia, that's when his work changed. She was a folk singer in the Village and very pretty. His artist friends abandoned him then."

"Jealous?"

"Some. But it was also him. He stopped coming to the happenings. He wanted to spend time just with her. Not share her with the group. Like that."

Diane poured an orange liquer into a small glass.

"Are you sure?" she asked, holding up the glass.

"No thanks."

"Clifford wanted only one woman. He wasn't interested in playing around after he met her. He really loved Livia. This was too bourgeois for the group. Not hip enough. So they attacked him. Vicious. It was awful to see. Even if they wanted to be part of the scene, they couldn't. Clifford was dead to them. It was shameful, really. I was the only one of the group who remained friends with him," Diane said. She shifted in the seat and rested her back against the wall. The only righteous one, Greg thought sarcastically. "Do you want some coffee? I think there's some I can make."

"I'm good, thanks," Greg said, "really."

"Clifford took the snub very hard. So he reciprocated in kind. He stopped talking to nearly everyone. He and Livia turned inward, completely content with themselves. Livia continued singing in clubs, but they never hung out with anyone else, at least not the old crowd. He stopped submitting his poems for publication. But, you know, I liked Livia as much as Clifford. I could see why he loved her. They were so much alike, really. And I enjoyed the company of both of them until they moved to Europe."

"So he talked to you?"

"Yes. I would go to the coffeehouses to hear Livia," Diane said. "I thought she deserved more recognition than she received. She played Gerde's Folk City one time. It was sad, though. You know, no one was much interested in listening to folk music or any music any more. Dance to it, party to it, space out to it, fuck to it, anything but listen to it. So she was finished. But Clifford was always there. We always talked when we saw each other. It wasn't more than that, though. Not friends. In a year or so folk music was gone completely, so they were even more to themselves than ever. Recluses really."

Greg looked at Diane's legs. She kicked off her shoes.

"After I graduated from law school, I took a position with an international corporation and my work often took me to Europe. I heard that they had moved to Europe, so I managed to track them down and we resumed our friendship, acquaintanceship. Whenever I was nearby, I made sure to see them. It was once a year or so. But it was enough. I don't think they wanted more than that. And the best I could figure out, they didn't have any other friends. At least, I never met anyone else. They were very private. The two of them."

"Did Livia continue to sing in France?"

"I don't think so. I think she gave it up totally."

Diane explained that Livia's death, as could have been expected, left Clifford bereft.

"I'm not sure why he wanted to come home after she died. I guess after all those years in France with Livia he couldn't bear to be there without her. When he moved to New York, he asked me to be his lawyer and executor. He didn't have much, but he didn't want the state to get their hands on anything."

"No children, I suppose?" Greg asked.

Diane shook her head.

"They never talked about why they didn't have kids," she said. "Maybe there was no room for a third." Diane stood and held her back. "And you?" she asked, wincing as she rubbed her hip.

"Never married," Greg said.

"Gay?" she asked.

Greg laughed. "Hardly. My problem is that I like women too much." Perhaps at some other time he would tell her more.

"At least we have something in common," Diane said. She rose from her seat. "Well, I have to start sorting through things. There are documents and unpaid bills."

"Can I look around?" Greg asked.

He looked at the pictures on the table, then went into the adjoining room. On a nightstand, next to the bed, was a photograph of Livia. Between it and the window was only one other piece of furniture in the room, a floor-to-ceiling lawyer's cabinet with oblong glass doors that lifted up to open that was filled with teapots.

"I always met Clifford in the living room," Diane said. "There was never a reason for me to be here before. It feels like I'm trespassing, you know." Diane looked the pots through the little windows. "Livia loved tea," she said. "Clifford preferred coffee, but she only drank tea." Diane squatted to look at the lower shelves. "Now that I think about it, she did use several different pots. I had coffee with Clifford, but she always had tea with us. I know that she always brewed it, never a teabag. But I can't remember what pots the tea came in, but these," she said as she slid open one of the doors, "these are really beautiful. I had no idea that she was a collector."

Greg said, "I guess Clifford decided to ship them back to the States. They seem to be the only personal things in the apartment. Aside from the photos."

Diane took out a clay pot with Chinese writing on its fluted sides. On its lid were figures of a dragon and a phoenix.

"Please," Clifford said, as he took the pot from Diane.

One by one, they removed a pot, examined it and replaced it on the shelf. Under each of the pots was a note card with the date and place of purchase and something about the pot itself—its age, style, the kind of tea it was used for and a poetic phrase.

"His poems for Livia."

"You're the executor, Diane," Greg said as he admired the blue one with the white phoenix. "What are you going to do with them?"

"What do you think should happen? They don't look like they're very valuable."

"They were to Clifford and Livia," Greg said with a bit too much annoyance.

"See what I can sell on eBay and throw away the rest, I suppose."

"You would do that? It feels like a betrayal of the two them somehow. Separating them in death."

"They're lovely. But I don't do collectibles," she said. "I didn't expect that you'd to be sentimental, you know." Greg hadn't either. "If you want them, you can have them,"

Greg carefully removed each teapot from the display case, making sure to keep to keep the poem with its proper mate, wrapped them in newspaper, then placed them in packing boxes that Diane had brought with her. There were more than fifty teapots in all: porcelain, iron, silver, tin, glass, stone, terracotta and purple clay.

Greg had no idea what he was going to do with them either. He kept the packing boxes in a corner of his apartment, under the writing table he used for his work. A plan slowly took shape and before winter set in he knew what he was going to do. There was a pocket park near the loft where the happenings took place.

There, inspired by Rao's approach to art, Greg would randomly read aloud lines from Clifford's poems while smashing, throwing and battering the teapots to create something new. Then his column would be a reminiscence of Rao, resurrecting him—and Livia—, for a brief moment from the veil of forgetfulness into which they had fallen.

Months later, resolved to keep one for himself as a constant reminder of the vagaries of fame, Greg decided to keep the first one he picked from the box: a Japanese dobin-syle white teapot with hand-painted blue camellias and faint streaks of bamboo. When he removed the lid to brew some tea, as he was pouring in the steaming water, he noticed a piece of paper in the bowl of the pot. It was two seemingly unrelated sentences—something, he gathered, about Clifford and Livia. He took out another pot from the box, then another until every one was exposed. Each contained a piece of paper.

Greg laid out the papers on the floor of his apartment. One teapot contained Livia's birth certificate, another a part of letter sent from Clifford to Livia. In another teapot was a studio portrait of them in their wedding clothes. Initially, Greg thought the sentences were arbitrary, just snatches, but the more he looked, the more he thought that it was perhaps a code. He reassembled the scraps again and again, moving them about like jigsaw pieces, until a narrative, in fact, did emerge.

Clifford and Livia were half-brother and –sister. Like a good fabulist, Greg filled in the blanks of the story: Livia, born in Alabama, met Clifford when she moved to New York. Only after becoming lovers did they discover that they shared the same absentee father.

Since meeting Diane at Rao's apartment, Greg hadn't spoken to Diane. Now he phoned her.

"Did you know anything about this?" he asked. "Why didn't you tell me."

"I didn't know. There were hints here and there. I had my suspicions, but I didn't know. I wouldn't ask them."

"I'm shocked," Greg said. "I don't know what to make of this."

"I guess you have another book." She said this too quickly, with a little too much enthusiasm. "It's the kind of thing that you write about, isn't it? They were living on the border, weren't they?"

"Maybe they crossed it."

"It is fascinating."

"Yes. And disturbing."

"I didn't know you were judgmental."

"It doesn't bother you?"

"No. Should it? They loved each other. They didn't know it when they first fell in love. There are no children. So what's the problem?" She waited for a response. There was none. "I think it's kind of romantic. And ironic, too. Clifford was the only one in the group that defied convention until the end. It's funny, Greg. You turned out to be more bourgeois than me."

Diane called after Greg's column about Rao was published. The article, understated and reflective, was an admission of his carelessness with friends, the dropped connections, his reluctance to express gratitude, the ways in which we never know how we affect others.

"Lovely piece, Greg," Diane said. She asked after the book idea about Rao's life. "I think there's a great book here. Their secret is really shocking."

"Still thinking about it," he replied coldly.

Diane called and emailed a few more times inquiring about the book. Greg suspected that behind Diane's importuning was a pecuniary interest in resurrecting Rao's fame. He presumed she was the heir to all his work. Greg didn't call back or email her. Some people were worth leaving behind.

Eventually Diane stopped contacting him.

With the first snow scheduled for later that week, Greg gathered the teapot papers and went to the park across and there cut the paper into confetti-size shreds and rolled them between his fingers making them into tiny balls as he read Rao's poem from his college poetry anthology. As onlookers gathered, he offered them a "piece of history." A few took the balls of—single letters, smudges, phrases, words, a part of an official seal, dates, place names, a woman's name, a man's name with a line drawn through.

The sun disappeared behind the tall buildings and the air turned cold in the twilight. Greg walked back to his apartment, scattering the remaining balls of paper behind him, like Hansel and Gretel trailing breadcrumbs as they walked into the woods, hoping to find their way home later in the day. He couldn't bring himself to smash the teapots.

DEEP WELL

$\mathcal{D}$EEP WELL, A TOWN IN THE HIGH PRAIRIE NOT far from the Canadian border, reached its zenith during WWII, when troop trains from Chicago filled with soldiers on their way to the Pacific Theater stopped for refueling before continuing across the Rockies en route to Seattle. Lillian, a junior member of the Red Cross, served hot coffee and donuts made in her family's kitchen to thousands of men, one of whom, Pvt. Stanley Wicks, a 20-year-old, fell in love with her on a November morning. A month later he found himself stationed at Army camp post offices, first in the South Pacific and later in the Philippines. It was easy for him to regularly send letters to the young woman whose address had been written on a paper napkin, and it was easy for Lillian to fall in love with the young man who touched her heart with his weekly solicitations.

Stanley Wicks came to Deep Well after the war to ask Lillian's father for permission to marry her. Not only did Mr. Robert agree to the proposal, he made one of his own.

"Why don't you and Lillian settle right here," he said. "Lillian's an only child. There are no boys to take over. I can teach you what you need to know about farming. We'll build another house for you and Lillian over by the river. This property has been in my family for more than seventy-five years. And it will be yours and Lillian's to continue when I'm gone."

When he arrived in Montana to propose to Lillian, Stanley imagined that he and Lillian would return to Michigan where he would take a job in the Ford plant or maybe in the US Post Office and he would get a G.I. mortgage and buy a house in the suburbs for his new family. At first, he didn't know what to say to Lillian's father's proposition. His parents were immigrants and his father and uncles all worked in factories in the Mid-west, but after sitting with his future father-in-law in the downtown bar over a beer, he said yes.

*T*his wasn't her dream. Lilian didn't want to say no to Stanley and neither could she refuse her father's offer, not after Stanley had already accepted it. She wouldn't begin her marriage as a disagreeable wife.

When the troop trains had stopped in Deep Well, Lillian imagined herself taking the rails to some far place. She wanted away from the small town and the drifting snow and blistering summers; she wanted more excitement than church suppers and square dances. She wanted to see for herself what she saw in *National Geographic*. She had read Edward Thorndike's 1937 study in *Reader's Digest*. In this poll young recipients of government relief were asked how much they would have to be paid to accept various experiences. A tooth pulled; $4,500; a toe amputated,

$57,000; eat a worm, $100,000; live the rest of your life on a farm in Kansas, ten miles from any town, $300,000. Kansas, she thought. She could settle for that.

Over the years, she tried to hide her disappointment. One by one shops and stores in Deep Well closed, both her parents died and the nearest neighbors grew even more distant as family farms were sold to corporate owners. Stanley promised that when the last of the children were grown and the farm could be safely passed on, they would retire to Arizona or California, but this became increasingly unlikely as profits from their farm diminished. Production costs increased and it became nearly impossible to compete against corporate farms that could take advantage of economies of scale. The Wicks owed more on the loan for their combine harvester than they had saved in a lifetime, and none of their children wanted to take up farming.

Lillian's disappointment didn't extend to Stanley. She loved him more now than when she read his letters from the Pacific; he was a devoted husband and a good father to their children. But her desire for something greater than the circumscribed life in Deep Well was passed on to her children. The older boys went to the state university. The first remained in Bozeman, where he taught Phys Ed, while the other managed a year-round resort in the mountains for the wealthy owned by a famous newscaster. Their daughter left home for Minneapolis after graduating from high school.

Kent, the youngest of the four, wanted to do something purposeful with his life, in the way that Deep Well had once done something noble when the troop trains passed through. His parents' marriage proved to him that helping others could lead to a life full of love, although perhaps not happiness, at least in the usual sense of that word. When he told his parents that he wanted to be a doctor, they encouraged him.

"We need doctors in this part of the country," his father said. The nearest doctor was a two-hour drive away and a hospital much further than that.

Kent wanted more of a challenge than being a family physician in a remote region, no matter how important this might be, or working in a community hospital in Havre or Chinook. He was inspired by the stories in *Popular Science* that arrived at their Deep Well home, reports about medical advances and breakthroughs expected in medicine in the near future—heart transplants, cancer cures, the elimination of all childhood diseases. He could be of most use in a large hospital or doing research at a university.

Lillian smiled wanly when Kent said that he wanted to go to the top college that would accept him. He had spoken to the guidance counselor at school and they decided that a military academy was his best choice.

"The education's better than at a state school," he explained to his parents. His father was uncertain.

"We can afford State," his father said. Kent knew the family's finances well enough. He would go to State, if there were no other choice.

"There's no tuition at the academy," Kent said, "and there's no fee for room and board. The whole thing is free. And then they'll send me to medical school."

"Are you sure you can deal with them telling you what to do?" his father asked. "I didn't like the army much. In fact, the only thing I liked about it was meeting your mother."

"I'll be an officer," Kent explained. "I start out as a captain when I finish medical school."

"I hope the war is over before you have to serve," Stanley said.

Kent knew the story about the troop train, so putting on a uniform didn't seem such a bad thing to do. He willingly accepted the terms of the bargain: after graduation, if his grades warranted it, the military would send him to medical school in return for what amounted to early years of his career as an army officer.

"It's tough getting in," Kent said.

There won't be many more conversations with our son, Lillian thought. Stanley had never returned to Detroit, and she no more expected Kent to return to Deep Well. She wanted to say, "Going away will be forever." Instead, she said, repeating an Irish saying she was fond of, "A hundred years can't repair a moment's loss of honor."

*T*he two nominations to West Point from the state's Congressional representative that year were from the same high school. Kent and Norman graduated with nearly identical grade point averages; Kent was the captain of the swimming team and Norman the captain of the football team. Their SAT scores matched within a few points, with Kent receiving a higher score on the math portion but Norman scoring a few more on the English section.

Kent didn't much like Norman. Maybe it was because they competed for the same girls. But it was more than that. Norman wanted too much to be like Kent. Whatever Kent liked, Norman developed a liking for—tastes in music, styles of dress, favorite TV shows and sports teams. Kent found Norman's behavior unseemly. It was no surprise, then, that when Kent wrote to the Congressional Representative for a letter of recommendation, Norman did the same. It rankled him. When he allowed himself to look at his feelings, he hoped that Norman would be rejected.

It was unusual for the academy to admit two students from one high school in the same year, but there were few applications from Montana when Kent and Norman applied. Despite the warnings of the John Birch Society about communism taking away their freedom, and the American Legion railing against cowardly draft-dodging war protesters, and politicians linking marijuana and anarchy, and churches preaching the spirit to resist godlessness, young men of Montana were taking more cues from Haight-Ashbury than Last Chance Gulch, Helana's main street; a few from the area had gone across the Canadian border to avoid the draft.

No other superior candidates from the state applied to the academy. Soon after graduation from the regional high school, Kent and Norman took a bus to Great Falls, changed planes in Minneapolis for New York, and another bus ride 50 miles along the Palisades along the Hudson River.

Kent was relieved when he and Norman were housed in separate dorms and assigned to separate companies. He saw Norman in the mess hall, where they sat in silent discipline at opposite sides of the great room. The less Kent saw of Norman the less he disliked him.

Kent easily adapted to the routine of a cadet: rigorous academics, a regimented schedule, close-cropped hair, following orders without question, and indoctrination. Without the distraction of females, he focused on his grades and did better than he had hoped, finding himself near the top of the freshman class. He felt certain that he would be the doctor he dreamed of becoming.

The call from home came as a surprise. His father had shown no signs of illness. Within a month of the diagnosis of colon cancer, he was dead.

As they sat in the house after the funeral, the children talked to Lillian about her future. Everyone but Lillian agreed that she had to leave the farm. She would be OK, she said. Her son in Bozeman invited her to move close to him. He and his wife lived in a trailer, but they could find an apartment for her nearby. There was an active club at one of the churches in town where she could meet other widows, he said. The daughter was planning to move from Minneapolis after a bitter divorce and said that she was packing for New Orleans. Kent smelled a hint of marijuana in her hair and liquor on her breath. Lillian's other son said that he needed to get back to work; the resort was in the midst of expansion and needed his attention.

Lillian said she would manage somehow, for the while, by hiring hands or renting out the fields to neighbors.

"You're going to have to sell the farm sometime," Kent said.

He knew that she wouldn't leave. Her roots were too deep, especially with Stanley now buried next to her parents in the graveyard of Deep Well Lutheran Church. She couldn't imagine anywhere else to spend eternity.

"You'll be too lonely, Mom," Kent said to her, as they sat at the kitchen table after the others returned to their own homes. "You can't stay here by yourself."

"I'm not going to let you do this," Lillian said to Kent, running her fingers through his hair. "You have to stay in school. I'm not going to let you come home. Your life isn't here. You see what's happening all around. You can't return to emptiness. I wish that I had gone when I was your age, with your father. I'm not going to let you regret making this decision."

Kent looked up from his coffee cup and watched tears roll down his mother's cheeks. He wiped them dry.

"Who will take care of you?" he asked.

*T*houghts of his mother were close to Kent, as he received weekly letters from Deep Well, always written on Sunday evenings after Lillian returned from the church social. He phoned home, as often as he could, but the lines of cadets waiting at the pay phone were so long that he often had to return to his dorm, in order to meet curfew, before talking to his mother.

Kent had more contact with Norman during the spring semester, when Norman asked Kent to study with him. At first, Kent was reluctant, but after nights together in the library and seeing that Norman truly was a weak student, Kent felt useful, if not a little smug. Norman was struggling with his academics.

"I don't know if I can succeed here," Norman said. "I think I've gotten in over my head. This is crazy hard."

While he thought that Norman was probably right in his assessment, he offered encouragement.

"I don't think I'm cut out for the military," he added. "I really don't like it. It's not what I thought it would be."

"Then maybe you should leave," Kent said.

"I was thinking about that. Maybe going to New York City."

"To do what? Don't you think you should graduate from college?"

"I don't know. Or I could head up to Vermont, you know, just drop out for awhile."

"You'll be drafted. Then you'll be in the army as an enlisted man. Don't you think you're better off being an officer?"

Kent heard rumors that Norman associated with cadets who used drugs, a group that, it seemed, wanted West Point's parade grounds to become Strawberry Fields. Kent stayed apart, never participating in activities that would bring dishonor. He accepted the conditions for his admittance and thought that flouting the rules was dishonest. The academy's strict and rigid honor code— no excuses, no exceptions, no second chances; any violation, no matter how minor, meant automatic expulsion; any cadet who knows of a violation must report it and failure to do so also meant automatic discharge—was something he agreed to when he raised his right hand.

"Come on," Kent said, as he pushed the calculus text towards Norman across the carrel table. "Let's go over the questions."

Throughout the semester, as Kent spent more time studying with Norman and seeing him struggle, he came to like him. Perhaps it had to do with familiarity—their shared experiences at the regional high school, his knowing Kent's family, having lived on a farm struggling to keep from bankruptcy. Whatever irritation Kent had felt towards Norman dissipated and he began to feel like a sibling helping a struggling, younger brother. Helping Norman to stay in West Point would distract him from thoughts about his mother and relieve some of his unease about her situation.

Nothing came easy to Norman. While Kent breezed through most subjects, his friend struggled with them all. But with Kent's persistence and cajoling, Norman completed his assignments and passed his exams.

"You did well on that paper," Kent said as they sat in Norman's dormitory. Kent picked up a stapled sheaf of papers on top of Norman's chemistry text.

"It was OK," he said. Norman took it from Kent.

"A B+. What's wrong with that? Was that for your World History class?"

The more enthusiasm Kent expressed the quieter Norman became. Kent stopped when Norman cupped his face in his hands as he sat on the bed.

"Well," Norman said, "this wasn't a subject you could help me with. You haven't taken that class yet."

"Who did help you?" As soon as he said this, Kent wished he hadn't. There was no need to embarrass Norman. But when Norman answered, Kent's discomfort turned to anger.

"You did what?"

"It's no big deal," Norman said as he picked up his head. "Jesus, it's only one paper. It's not like a final or something," he said in a harsh whisper. He took a few short breaths, then continued calmly. "Besides, everyone does it. Come on, tell me you've never copied a paper."

Kent didn't answer. "You know the code," he said instead. "You promised when you took your oath."

"This isn't the Boy Scouts."

"Are you kidding, Norman? Doesn't your *word* mean anything?"

"Staying in school means something," Norman said. "You do what you got to do."

"You can't let this slide," Kent said forcefully. "You have to turn yourself in."

"I can't do that. That'll be the end of me."

"Come on."

"This isn't the end of the world, Kent. The code is unreasonable. It's like being executed for stealing a loaf of bread. It's wrong what I did. But I had to. Now just shut up about it, OK?"

Kent stayed awake all night with the lights off, going over his options in his mind. The next day Kent reported to the Commanding Officer and resigned from the academy. Later that day he went to the CO again, this time to report Norman's plagiarism.

"*I* couldn't just report him, Mom," he said to Lillian. "I had to resign first before telling the CO."

His mother sighed.

"I would never know if I was reporting him because I wanted to save myself or whether I was doing it because it was the right thing. Once I knew that he had copied the paper, I had to turn him in. If I didn't and they found out, then I'd get expelled. But that shouldn't be the reason. I needed to report it because plagiarism is wrong, the army can't have officers who are cheaters. It shouldn't be that I acted out of fear that I would be caught not saying anything."

"But this way you're out, too. So what did you gain?"

"I spent the night thinking about this. I had to do it this way. If I just told, I'd never know why I did it. I had to do it for the right reason. If I was going to turn him in, it couldn't be to save my own skin. If that's what it was, then the honor code doesn't make sense. The only way to know if I really believed in the system was to take myself out of it completely. Once I did that, I knew for sure. Cheating isn't right and the academy had to know that Norman wasn't honest. Cadets are going to become officers and have men's lives in their hands. They can't be cheats. They have to be men that you have complete trust in."

Lillian brushed the front of her housedress.

"They would know that about Norman whether you resigned or not."

"But I wouldn't know why I had done it. And that was important to me, that it was an important value I was defending."

She had raised a boy with too much integrity, she thought. Then she leaned across the table and put her hand on his shoulder.

"It's alright, Mom. I'll be OK. I'll apply to State. It'll be OK."

His grades were outstanding. He would be accepted at State, he was sure. Kent began to think about the hospital in Great Falls. Doctors were needed in Montana as much as anywhere. Perhaps this would turn out to be for the best after all.

"Sure it will be," his mother said.

Kent bore no grudge against Norman. He took his mother's hand and smiled. She didn't and thought, 'My boy's too good.'

THE HARDER RIGHT

$\mathcal{J}$ASON WAS A SOUND SLEEPER, BARELY STIRRING before morning. His college roommate described this as "the sleep of the dead," but really it was that Jason had an easy conscience, ending the day secure in knowing that, if not having *succeeded* in being a good person, at least certain that he had tried to live up to his moral standards. Harsh words, unkind thoughts, being less than generous and too judgmental, putting himself before others—all this bothered Jason, but compared to many of his friends from the neighborhood or other students on campus, he felt that, on balance, he was a decent person, good enough for the moment, and, at least, trying to be better. Whatever his faults and limitations, he had never deliberately hurt anyone and what laws he broke were negligible. Jason had a clear conscience and, therefore, untroubled nights.

When asked about his dreams, he said that while he *had* dreams, he rarely remembered them. He could recall only the embarrassing, sexual ones in detail, which he didn't reveal to anyone.

Mostly, though, his dreams were of flying and getting lost, or forgetting that it was the end of the semester and there was a final that day, and disappointing someone (his father?) with a failing grade—the usual stuff of dreams, but even these were insipid, hardly a cause for introspection or concern.

This night was different. When he awoke, he found the cotton top sheet twisted and wet. The details of the dream were as vivid now as they had been when he was asleep and the disquieting feelings associated with the dream stayed with him throughout the day. Despite his uneasiness, the more he thought about it the more re-assured he became. He went over the scene again.

He had done the right thing; he was certain of it.

In his dream, Jason stood on a hill and saw in the gully below him a freight train careering down the track; on the other side of a long bend a group of teenagers, with beer bottles in their hands, pushed and shoved each other, and in their horse play they were oblivious to the on-rushing train.

Jason called for them to get off the tracks, "There's a train coming!" As often happens in a dream, no sound came out of his mouth. He tried to get the engineer's attention by throwing rocks at the train, but he failed at that, too. Jason waved his hands, he whistled and shouted until his throat was sore, but the train kept speeding and the teenagers kept up their antics on the tracks.

Jason was going to witness the deaths of a dozen teenagers who were foolishly partying where they shouldn't have been. Looking down from the hilltop, just as the train entered the curve, he saw a rail spur. If the train took the side shunt, their lives would be spared. He was about to turn away in horror, unable to alter the scene unfolding before him, but now behind a scrubby bush he found a railroad switch. If he pushed the lever to the right, the train would be sent down the spur, avoiding hitting the teenagers. He grabbed the control but just before throwing the switch, Jason saw a worker fixing the track on the spur. There would be no time to warn the repairman. Jason watched the train from his perch on the hill, having only a second to decide whether to throw the switch.

Although he felt that he had done the right thing, still the dream haunted him. Every so often he would recall it, when hearing about a difficult choice made by someone in the news and could feel the dream all over again. Mostly, though it was forgotten.

*T*he planes struck the buildings when Jason was in school.

When his class was canceled and the college evacuated, he walked into the air gray from the smoke of the smoldering buildings just a few blocks away. People covered with ghost-like ash staggered by in silence, others sat on the curb, not knowing where to go, wondering what had happened. The country had been attacked, he heard from an apparition scuttling by. The only sounds were sirens; the city had gone mute. Later he couldn't remember who had stood with her arms around him or whose hand he clutched or who walked miles over the bridge to Brooklyn with him.

Jason returned to Manhattan the next day and found Washington Square filled with photographs of the missing, pleas and poems and commemorations of the dead; the nearby fire station was draped with black and purple banners. Jason wanted to donate blood, but none was needed. There were few victims to care for. He wanted to volunteer—for something, anything—but he had no needed skill to offer. He, like many others, applauded the firefighters when they drove by in their trucks.

When classes resumed, his mind drifted. He found his courses pointless and he couldn't concentrate. The tragedy changed Jason's desire to become a sports commentator or possibility a music promoter. These were put behind and he thought of them as being childish and trivial things. He didn't know what he was going to do after graduation, but whatever it was it had to be consequential. The firefighters were inspiring and even the dull duty of the National Guard at Penn Station seemed noble. His real heroes, though, were the men on United Flight 93—"Don't worry, we're going to do something"—who, in a failed attempted to prevent the hijacking, rushed the terrorists on the fourth plane that crashed in a field in Pennsylvania.

The attack reshaped Jason's values. He thought about how lucky he had been to get a scholarship to NYU, a school far beyond his parents' means. While in high school, he avoided fights and during the summers he stayed to himself in his apartment. He was glad that he was afraid of violence. He was happy to leave his neighborhood behind when the scholarship allowed him to live in a dormitory. He saw what violence did to his friends and he vowed that he would never use force or carry a knife or gun. Words, reason and intelligence—that's what was needed, not more bloodshed. How could violence solve the problem of violence? If he had the word for it, he would have called himself a pacifist. But his view shifted that September. There is no reasoning with people who want to murder you; there is no persuading a fanatic.

The fight against Al Qaeda was a just war and he had an obligation to do whatever he could, not simply to prevent them from killing more innocent people, but to bring freedom to others. If ever a war was right, this was it. His non-violence before 9/11 was a rationalization for his cowardice.

When he graduated from college that May, over the strong objections of his father, who remembered his own brother's death in Vietnam, Jason joined the military.

*D*espite the army's encouraging him to become an officer, Jason rejected the commission. He wanted no part of making decisions that affected the lives of others. He wasn't seeking a military career; the army was a placeholder until he could figure out what he really wanted to do with his life, where best to put his new-found convictions. It was an opportunity to think about his future precisely because he didn't have to make decisions, a luxury that would be denied if he were an officer. Meanwhile, he would be of use to his country and test himself.

Jason adjusted quickly to the basic training routine. Being told what to do, what to wear, how to wear it, what and when to eat made life simpler, something he enjoyed. Within the first two days he memorized the Army General Orders and the next week he was designated temporary sergeant. He readily learned drill formations, field stripped his weapons in the dark, and qualified as an expert marksman.

To his surprise, the Army Values Handbook was useful in providing him with a way of understanding his activities. At night, as he sat on his bunk polishing his boots and folding his clothes in his locker, he tried to make sense of "loyalty, duty, respect, selfless service, honor, integrity and personal courage." More than any course he took in college, he found the book of practical use, as he memorized the page devoted to ethical decision-making— identify the problem, examine the choices, choose that course most consistent with Army values and regulations, and carry out the plan.

Jason expected that the army would teach him how to defend himself and how to kill, but not to get him to think about ethical values. In the Handbook he read the West Point Cadet Prayer —"Make us to choose the harder right instead of the easier wrong"; and this from a former Army Chief of Staff—"The essence of duty is acting in the absence of orders or direction from others, based on an inner sense of what is morally and professionally right." Without effort, he memorized that a "soldier displays integrity when he or she always acts according to what he or she knows to be right, even at personal cost; possesses a high standard of moral values and principles; shows good moral judgment and demonstrates consistent moral behavior; avoids the wrong and stands up for what is right; abides by principles." But what did this really mean? What was his inner sense of morality? Did he even have one? And what was he really supposed to do if there was a conflict between his principles and orders he received? His values were clear, but he wasn't at all certain about his principles. And most troubling was that he had no idea how he would act if he found himself in combat, when there was no time to mull over philosophical fine points.

After basic training, Jason decided to push himself further; he volunteered for the Special Forces.

Questions about his life's goals and values persisted when he arrived in southern Afghanistan, as part of Operation Enduring Freedom. He wasn't in the country more than a week when the dream he had while at NYU returned. For the next several days, he replayed the scene. Now he reviewed his choice in light of the decision-making approach in the Soldier's Handbook. The problem was clear enough: the train couldn't be stopped and it was going to kill the carousing teenagers unless it could be diverted. He had two choices. He could do nothing and let them die or throw the switch, sending the train down the spur to kill the workman. To do nothing would mean a half-dozen dead; shunting the train onto the spur meant one death. He was sure that he had done the right thing. He wouldn't watch and say that it was all in the hands of God, a matter of fate. This would be a rationalization for inaction. He accepted the proposition that by doing nothing, he would have been responsible for a half-dozen deaths, just as had become responsible for the death of the one man by throwing the switch. This was the better of two bad choices. He accepted the burden of free will, the necessity of a guilty conscience.

His army indoctrination had confirmed the instinct that he expressed in the dream. Minimizing casualties was the right thing to do. Jason believed that killing was sometimes a necessary evil and the fight against terrorists was a just war.

But he was also angry that in his dream he found himself in a situation, not of his own doing, from which there was no escape. Whatever his choice, he would feel guilty for having caused the deaths of one or more people. If the teenagers hadn't been so careless, if they hadn't been drinking and foolish, the workman wouldn't have had to die. They shouldn't have been there in the first place. But they were. That much he couldn't change.

$\mathcal{J}$ason's company was sent to the mountains in the Pashtun area where the Taliban had regrouped after their initial losses at the hands of the American and NATO troops. The men who had so ruthlessly ruled the country and conspired with Al Qaeda now promised to take control again and renew their holy war.

American intelligence suspected the village of Spin Kundi was a key site for the Taliban. Several commanders of the resurgent Taliban had taken hold there and were responsible for ordering rocket attacks against government outposts and NATO bases. Although they wore no uniforms and represented no government, the terrorists were enemy combatants engaged in war.

Jason's four-man squad was dropped by helicopter fifty miles from their base and about twenty miles away from Spin Kundi, which lay across desolate mountains. They were to carry out a reconnaissance mission. Since the insurgents lived amongst the civilians in the village, the coalition forces were reluctant to attack. The Taliban were using civilians as shields. Jason's commando squad was to secretly reconnoiter Spin Kundi from a nearby distance and provide the Americans with information to ensure that the Taliban could be precisely targeted by the Air Force, thereby hoping to minimize civilian deaths.

After breaking camp the following morning, the squad separated a mile from Spin Kundi. As Jason approached the crest of a hill overlooking the town, he heard the tinkling of bells. Jason crouched and aimed his rifle at the noise that grew louder behind him.

Startled—

there

children?
—yes, three
children, girls
tending goats.

Their hair was matted with gray mountain dust. The girls stood barefoot, their dresses worn pieces of canvas, not one taller than the goats they herded. They saw Jason, stood still, one clutching a plastic water bottle to her chest. Jason kept his rifle trained on the chest of one closest to him, then certain that the girls were alone, he lowered his rifle and, keeping his distance, greeted them in the local language, the only phrase he knew in their tongue.

The goatherds seemed unfazed by the stranger with the rifle. This, Jason, thought is what you are supposed to do when confronted with a wild animal. Show no fear, say nothing.

The shaggy goats grazed on a patch of weeds growing around an outcropping of rock, some huddled around the girls' legs.

"We have a situation here," Jason whispered as he held the transceiver in one hand, not taking his eyes off the girls. "What the hell am I going to do with them?"

The squad's mission required they travel light, so while they had some items in their backpacks, Jason didn't have enough material to restrain all three. The other squad members couldn't join Jason without risking exposing their positions.

There was a quick discussion about disabling the girls by shooting them in the legs but their screams would easily be heard in the town. The squad quickly concluded that they had only two alternatives: the first, let the goatherds go and risk that the girls would reveal the squad's location when they reached town and, therefore, risk being attacked by the Taliban.

Second, "We kill them."

They put it to a vote.

The goatherds eyes were still downcast as he raised his rifle, placed his finger on the trigger and aimed at the head of the oldest. The shot will be muffled by the silencer. He will be the only person to hear the pop no longer than a dropped pebble on the hardscrabble earth.

"Turn around! Turn around!"

The sharp sound of Jason's command frightened the girls. Their eyes widened and all three began to wail. Jason released his finger from the trigger and waved the rifle towards Spin Kundi.

"Get the fuck out of here!" he yelled. "Go, go."

The girls remained motionless. They couldn't understand him. Jason stood and moved to shove them in the direction of Spin Kundi. His step forward made him like a predator about to pounce on its prey. The girls dashed towards the village, their banshee-like wails ringing in Jason's ears as they raced past him.

They needed to abort their mission. They called the base for immediate evacuation. A helicopter would arrive in ten minutes. As the squad made its way to their rendezvous point and waited, Jason heard the thud of the helicopter approaching. Before it reached them, insurgents surrounded them and attacked the squad. Jason rolled into a small gully. By the time he was rescued, the Taliban had killed his comrades. Jason was evacuated to the base with serious wounds to his back and legs.

*U*pon his discharge from the army, Jason returned to college to graduate with a doctorate in clinical psychology. He specializes in therapy with children who have had a parent killed in combat.

Like many other veterans, he refuses to talk about his wartime experiences. And if anyone were to ask about his dreams, Jason would say, "I don't remember anything."

AUTHOR'S NOTES

Passing Stranger: This situation came from a brief item in the news about a rabbi in the South who was the object of scorn because of his decision not to officiate at a funeral for a man who had refused to join the congregation.

Love the One You're With: Several missionaries attempting to spirit children out of Haiti after the massive 2010 earthquake were arrested. The legitimacy of a number of agencies that specialize in overseas adoptions has been questioned.

See American missionaries charged with kidnapping: http://abcnews.go.com/WN/haiti-earthquake-american-missionaries-arrested-kidnapping-children-proper/story?id=9736257

Lemon: A minister I knew adopted an older, difficult child. Soon after returning the boy, he resigned from the church. I also worked with families where conflicting versions of serious accusations against a family member were presented.

Shila: Self-sacrfice is a high virtue in some religious communities. This is from a private correspondence with a Jain scholar: "A mentally unsound girl would not be allowed to fast by the Jain com-munity. Fasting is considered deeply pious and no one would ever consider one who fasts to be insane. But fasting is carried out only by those who are mentally sound. And physically healthy."

In the United States, millionaire Zell Kravinsky gave away most of his fortune and donated one kidney to a stranger. For a philosophical argument about what is reasonable to give, see: http://www.utilitarian.net/singer/by/20061217.htm

Shila's refrain echoes that of the inscrutable character in Herman Melville's "Bartleby, the Scrivener," who frustratingly said in response to every request, "I'd rather not." See novella: http://www.gutenberg.org/catalog/world/readfile?fk_files=3282775

Kartik's Last Letter: An African acquaintance of mine struggled with his promise to help bring relatives to the US and his disillusionment with life in America. Another African acquaintance would not be able to return to the US because of visa restrictions if he went home for his mother's funeral.

Coral Fish: Some fish change their sex under certain conditions. http://www.bio.davidson.edu/Courses/anphys/1999/Rice/Rice.htm

I wondered, what if such a change occurred in human society. The dilemma in the story comes from a question considered in ethics, that is, whether motive or outcome is the measure of morality. For biblical commentary see: http://bible.cc/matthew/5-28.htm

The specific problem faced by the protagonist was suggested by Saul Smilansky's book *10 Moral Paradoxes*.

Girls in Paradise: UNESCO awarded a multi-million dollar endowment for research in the life sciences given by the president of Equatorial Guinea even though he has been accused by human rights groups as being a corrupt dictator. http://www.bbc.co.uk/news/world-africa-18857604

Naming university buildings after wealthy felons is controversial. http://www.mindingthecampus.com/forum/2007/07/honoring_criminals_on_campus_1.html

The Train to Amsterdam: An acquiantance told me that in 1938 his family in Vienna needed to decide whether to trust an employee in his father's factory who had become the local Nazi Youth leader when he offered to personally accompany the then-boy on a train to neutral Holland.

Black Ice: Tzuetan Todorou, in *Facing the Extreme: Moral Life in the Concentrations Camps*, tells the story of a young woman in Nazi Europe whose love for her mother led her to voluntarily join a line that she knew was taking them to a death camp.

(E)ruction (D)isorder: Sometimes manufacturers know their products are unsafe. http://www.nytimes.com/1988/07/24/magazine/into-the-mouths-of-babes.html?pagewanted=all&src=pm

In Treasured Teapots: A student told me about her aunt and uncle who had married each other and later learned that they were brother and sister who had been separated at birth. They revealed their secret to their family after many years. A similar story was reported in the press.

http://www.nydailynews.com/news/world/twin-brother-sister -marry-article-1.343118

Deep Well: A person I know faced this problem while at West Point and made a similar decision. He was subsequently reinstated, graduated from the academy and eventually retired from the army as an honored physician. See an article on West Point's honor code at: http://www.wcl.american.edu/journal/lawrev/27/ coyne.pdf

The Harder Right: The dream sequence is known as the "trolley problem," a much discussed thought experiment created by philosopher Philippa Foot. Philosophical discussion of this scenario can be found in Michel J. Sandel's *Justice: What's the Right Thing to Do?* and Kwame Anthony Appiah's *Experiments in Ethics.*

See the Army Values at: http://www.army.mil/values/index.html

The combat situation described closely resembles that of Navy SEAL Marcus Luttrell, which he recounts in his book *Lone Survivor: The Eyewitness Account of Operation Redwing and the Lost Heroes of SEAL Team 10*. See Luttrell's interview with Matt Lauer: http://www.youtube.com/watch?v=irC4K7Q4JCo

Michael Murphy, a squad member who died, was posthumously awarded the Medal of Honor. His father strongly disagrees with Luttrell's conclusion about what was the right course of action. See Dan Murphy's comments: http://www.nydailynews.com/news/book -prompts-battle-valor-article-1.220664

QUESTIONS FOR
DISCUSSION

Passing Stranger

1. Ali was the first and only Jew in the Buffalo County Clergy Association. Do you think that Ali was fully accepted by her Christian colleagues?

2. Do you think Ali did the right thing in rejecting the caller's request to officiate at his father's funeral? Why or why not?

3. In what ways do you think that her colleagues' reaction was a difference between Jewish and Christian attitudes towards the afterlife?

4. Do you think Ali's reaction to the caller was a matter of principle, a practical decision or a rash one due to frayed nerves?

5. Professions carry duties that go beyond personal choices. What was Ali's duty? Did she fulfill it?

6. Several things made Ali odd: her name, being a woman in a male dominated profession, being single where being married was

the norm, being the only Jew in the clergy association, being cosmopolitan in a rural area. How do you think this affected the way people viewed her decision to refuse to officiate at the funeral?

7. Do you think Ali's congregants and the Christian community had different reasons for their rejection of her?

8. Do you think Ali did the right thing by resigning her post? Why or why not?

9. Do you think Ali would have made a different decision if she had been married?

10. How do you interpret the story's title, "Passing Stranger"? In what ways does being a stranger affect Ali?

Love the One You're With

1. Thea and Marcus decided to get married in a religious ceremony. Do you think this was right even though they weren't especially religious? Why or why not?

2. When people marry, they often have a picture-perfect idea of the life ahead of them. Do you think this is setting themselves up for disappointment?

3. Do you think that Thea's and Marcus's parents' deaths prompted them to seek a fertility clinic?

4. Sex became a chore for Thea and Marcus. Do you think that when sex becomes a duty to be performed, marriage itself becomes a chore?

5. Marcus finds himself increasingly suspicious of Suffer the Children adoption service. Do you think that the different motives that Thea and Marcus have towards adoption predisposes

them to trust or distrust the service? In what ways do our desires interfere with being objective?

6. Do you think it was right for Marcus to insist on visiting the orphanage after the earthquake? What do you think were his reasons for going?

7. A woman stands silently when Marcus receives a bundle with the child's belongings. Who do you think this woman was? Does it matter? Should Marcus and Thea try to find out?

8. Marcus initially doesn't want to take the new child but quickly gives in. In leaving with the child Marcus is breaking Haitian law and faces breaking other laws in the US. Is it right to break the law?

9. Marcus and Thea will have to keep the circumstances of their child's adoption secret. How do you think they should deal with telling their daughter the facts surrounding her adoption?

10. Marcus returns not with the child he went to adopt but the one thrust upon him. Do you think that love comes from being with the one you are with?

Lemon

1. Roseline tells Walter that his decision isn't his alone to make. Do you think that decisions should be jointly made? Who else should be included in the decision? Who else will be affected by his decision?

2. When Walter came to the Fairview church, he wasn't especially popular. Roseline and her late husband were early supporters of Walter and made it possible for him to succeed. Does Walter have a special obligation to her because of that?

3. Walter held himself out as an example of Christian living. Give examples of this and do you agree with the choices he made?

4. Walter tries to balance his image and his personality. What toll do you think this took on him?

5. Walter challenged himself to comfort the afflicted and to afflict the comfortable. Should this be applied to his personal life as well?

6. Do you agree with Walter's arguments for adoption? What about his argument for adopting the most difficult of children?

7. Do you think Walter was bullying his wife into agreement? Should June have had a say as to whether to bring another child into the home?

8. When June saw the picture of her "older brother," she rejected him. Do you think it was prudent of Gwen and Walter to have treated June more affectionately than before? Would it have turned out differently if June was told that it was what it was and she should learn to cope with it?

9. What do you think happened to the missing ring? Do you believe June's accusation against Malcolm? How do you determine the truth when you have no direct evidence?

10. Do you think Malcolm would have been treated differently if he were their biological child? Is June's welfare the Braithwaite's primary concern? Is it ever right to give up on a child?

Shila

1. "Rationality and gentleness were the keys to raising a good child." Do you agree?

2. Does Shila make a good ethical argument for vegetarianism? Why or why not?

3. Do you think the death of Shila's father contributed to Shila's decisions? Why?

4. Shila makes many ethical decisions. What are they? Do you think Shila goes too far? What moral arguments can you present to counter Shila's?

5. When Shila decides to donate a kidney to a stranger, do you support her idea that all life is sacred? Is there a difference in what we owe to relatives and strangers? How do you justify your position?

6. "Rena had come to think that Shila's courage as compassion turned inside out, guilt disguised as conscience." Do you agree?

7. "Anger isn't a useful emotion," Shila says. Do you agree or disagree with her?

8. In the story we are told, "attachment is the source of evil." What does this mean? Do you agree?

9. At the end of the story, roles are reversed. Shila treats her mother as her own child. Do you agree with what Shila did? Why?

10. How do you distinguish between strictly adhering to ethical principles, fanaticism and mental illness?

Kartik's Last Letter

1. What promise did Kartik make? Is it right to make promises that may not be fulfilled?

2. "Today I received your letter from our beautiful home. How I miss it!" Why does Kartik start the letter nostalgically? Is this his true feeling?

3. Why did Somina send admission money to a college she barely knew, even though she had a brother who could have given her advice?

4. Kartik says, "there are many scams like this that take advantage of people like us." What does he mean?

5. Do you think that Kartik is doing the right thing when he tells his sister that he will claim that he is a lawyer or will use his friend's legal stationery to try to get the money back?

7. Do you think that it was right for Kartik to have promised his sister that he would come for her even though he did not have a real knowledge of where he was going?

8. Kartik opened his heart to his sister. Do you think it was wise of Kartik to burden his sister with all the truths of life in America?

9. Kartik tells Somina that he has to break the promise he made for her to follow him to America because of all the difficulties he has encountered. Do you think that this is Kartik's decision to make for Somina?

10. Kartik tells Somina that someone has to take care of Auntie. It is the family's responsibility. What do family members owe their elders? Whose interests should take priority, the young or the old?

Girls in Paradise

1. Axel, as director of the Committee for the Protection of Girls, wants to send Melita to attend a conference. Melita is reluctant to go, especially when a government whose human rights record was abysmal sponsored the conference. Do you think Axel

or Melita is right about attending a conference that is sponsored by the very people who themselves are responsible for the brutal treatment of girls?

2. Axel encourages Melita to take advantage of being in a beautiful place. He says, "You think it's selfish to enjoy yourself. It's the opposite. It's selfish to deprive yourself." He says, "Why not enjoy what you can when it is available?" Melita thinks this is a rationalization. Do you agree with Axel or Melita?

3. Kinzoni, the Minister of Social Services, invites Mellita to a party. What advice would you give her?

4. When Melita receives a note inviting her to meet privately with the president, she thinks she can't refuse. What would be the consequences of her refusing?

5. Melita snubs Chiku, the world-famous entertainer and president's goddaughter. Did she do the right thing?

6. Meltia decides that she won't tell Axel about the incident. Why does she plan to keep it secret?

7. Do you trust the president to keep his word regarding his gift to CPG?

8. If you were Axel, would you accept the money from the president? Do you think how money is gotten matters or is it more important that the money be put to good use?

9. Does the condition of naming centers after himself make any difference in accepting the president's gift?

10. Why does Melita get rid of the gems given to her by President Obengi? What would you do with them if they were given to you?

The Train to Amsterdam

1. Danilo rejects his family's view regarding Austria's future. Why does he hold his opinion so strongly?

2. "How can you live your life without trusting people?" Danilo asks rhetorically. What is your answer?

3. Danilo calls Michael Knauss "a fine boy" although he is a Nazi. Is it possible to be both a Nazi and a good person?

4. "Some young people do foolish things," Danilo says about Knauss. How should we judge bad things done by juveniles? When do we hold young people to adult standards?

5. When Danilo hears the knock at the door he says, "We can't refuse to answer. It may be someone who needs us." Was Danilo right?

When is it right to refuse to help?

6. Knauss says he wants to repay his family's debt to the Altmans. How do you judge Knauss and what he wants to do? How do you reconcile the goodness and evil that Knauss shows?

7. If you were the Altmans, would you let Rudolph leave on the train with Knauss? If you were Vera, would you leave without Danilo?

8. Vera and Danilo watched Rudolph at the station despite Knauss's directions not to go there. Was this worth the risk?

9. From the records Rudolph reads it seems as though Knauss was part of the Death Head unit that ran a concentration camp. If you were Rudolph, what would you think about Knauss? How would you evaluate him? What feelings would you have towards him?

10. Do you commend Knauss for his saving two of the three

Altmans, at great risk to himself? Or should he be condemned for his active participation in the Holocaust?

Black Ice

1. The Bahras are an oppressed minority. In what ways does this shape the relationships in Chania's family?

2. Chania is a modern girl growing up in a traditional family. In what ways is this expressed in her relation to her mother?

3. Khadroma chides Chania for being too smart for her own good. What does this mean? Is Chania a spoiled child?

4. Mother and daughter disagree about how to respond to prejudice. Kahdroma says to her daughter, "It was the same with your father and me when we were in school. That's the way it is." Do you agree with Kahdroma that it is best to accept life for what it is? Do you side with Chania, who speaks up? What kind of resistance is legitimate? Does it matter whether you are an adult or child?

5. Khadroma's sister and brother-in-law are planning to emigrate after their land has been expropriated. They want Khadroma and Chania to leave with them. Khardroma presents the idea to Chania. Should Khadroma leave the decision up to her daughter? What would you do if you were her?

6. Khadroma rejects Sopori, Chania's boyfriend, because he isn't a Bhara. Is Khadorma prejudiced? What do you think about intermarriage?

7. Chania says she isn't like her cousin, who was murdered because of his political involvement. She wants to make society better through her individual choices that ignore entrenched

animosities. Do you think that it is possible to separate personal and social ethics the way she wants?

8. Chania and her mother disagree about the power of love. What is your opinion?

9. Sopori wants to talk to Chania about the street violence but she doesn't want to spoil her wedding day. How far do you think Sopori should insist that Chania pay attention to what is happening on the street?

10. Chania joins her mother on what may be a death march. Why did she do this? Was it right to abandon Sopori? Was it the equivalent of committing suicide? Did she do the right thing?

(E)ruction (D)isorder

1. Durrel lives in a down and out city that is also home to very wealthy people. In what ways do you think seeing this wealth gap affects him?

2. If his life were to become easier, Durrell thought it would be a matter of luck. How much responsibility do we have for our lives and how much is luck?

3. Mineral water in Saratoga Springs runs free from taps around the city. Was it right for Durrell to charge for his water?

4. Does Durrell have a responsibility to check out his grandparents' claims for the water?

5. Although Durrell never believed in the cures claimed for the mineral waters, a claim is implied in the name he chose for the product. Is it right for him to imply such benefits for the water? What is a business's responsibility to consumers and what is the consumers' responsibility?

6. Durrell spoofs his own product in the video that goes viral. Is a parody a legitimate way to advertise or must advertising be informational?

7. After Sparkling Health Water becomes successful, Durrell dismisses his grandparents' contention that the product is dangerous. Why doesn't Durrell listen to his grandparents?

8. How diligent does Durrell need to be about his product before selling it to another company? Is it his responsibility to explain the problems associated with it or is it the buyer's responsibility to do a thorough investigation?

9. Durrell gets to live the high life by selling his company. What do you think about how he got his fortune? Do his grandparents have a responsibility to be public with the health problems?

10. Durrell doesn't break the law. Do you think that business has an ethical responsibility that exceeds what the law requires?

Coral Fish

1. The narrator says that his DNA has come back clean. How much can we—or want to—attribute our behavior and choices to DNA?

2. "I can't *make* myself feel sorry," the narrator says, although he acknowledges that he has done something wrong. What is the connection between thought and feeling? Are they linked in some way or are they completely separate?

3. The narrator says "my dilemma won't make sense" unless you understand his background better. Is it necessary to understand a situation fully before making judgments about it?

4. Do you agree that the problems listed by the narrator before the great change amount to "collective suicide'?

5. Are the problems society faces caused by human nature?

6. In this new world, there are many forms of government and people can move freely from country to country yet most stay put. The narrator says "most of us like what we have and where we are born. Mostly we stay put because we are convinced our way of doing things is the best." Do you agree?

7. The crime committed isn't considered a crime elsewhere. If this is so, how do you judge whether it should be a crime in the first place?

8. The narrator feels guilty that his good fortune came about because of someone else's misfortune. Do you consider this something to feel guilty about?

9. In the narrator's country, thoughts and feelings are as important as actions. Should people be judged by what's in their hearts and what they think or by what they do?

10. The narrator says that his parents were happy that he was born. The narrator asks, "Why can't I?" What is the answer to the question?

In Treasured Teapots

1. Greg says "a good childhood is one where parents leave you alone, where adults have their lives and children theirs." Do you agree?

2. What is it about Greg's childhood that makes him describe it as "breathing re-cycled and stale air"?

3. What do you think of Greg's road trip?

4. Greg describes an era when everything was questioned as "a time when life was freed by the imagination linked to courage." In your mind, is this a positive or negative?

5. Why do you think Rao was rejected by the other artists?

6. Greg regrets not contacting Rao. He wanted to tell him what an influence he had on his life. Why do you think Greg was neglectful?

7. What do you think is Diane's main reason for contacting Greg?

8. Did Diane have an obligation to preserve Rao's teapots?

9. Diane and Greg react to the Clifford and Livia's secret differently. How do you react and why?

10. What do you make of Greg's inability to smash the teapots.?

Deep Well

1. Stanley agrees to take over the Roberts' family farm, believing it will provide a better future for his new family. It isn't Lillian's dream, however. "She didn't want to say no to Stanley and neither could she refuse her father's offer." She didn't want to be a disagreeable wife. What do you think of her decision?

2. Kent's "parents' marriage proved to him that helping others could lead to a life full of love, although perhaps not happiness, at least in the usual sense of that word." Can life be happy, even though lacking self-fulfillment?

3. By attending the military academy, the best school given Kent's circumstances and ambitions, Lillian knew he wouldn't be coming back. He was leaving her to a life of loneliness. What does a mother owe her child? What do you think a son owes a mother?

4. After his father's funeral, Kent asks his mother, "Who will take care of you?" Which of the children should take responsibility for her?

5. Despite Kent not liking Norman, he helps him with his schoolwork. He seems to encourage Norman to leave the academy. What do you think is the proper stance for Kent to take towards Norman?

6. The academy's honor code allowed for no excuses, no exceptions and no second chances, no matter how minor the infraction. In addition, not reporting a violation was the same as having committed the violation. What do you think of such an honor system?

7. Norman justifies his copying a term paper by saying, "You do what you got to do," and adds, "everyone does it." Do you accept Norman's statements?

8. After Kent resigns from the academy, he turns in Norman. He says that he needed to know whether he reported Norman to prevent his own expulsion or because it was the right thing to do. What do you think of his reasoning?

9. The military relies upon officers being totally trustworthy. Do you think the academy's honor system fosters that in its future officers?

10. Kent acted to protect his own integrity but in so doing sacrificed his place at the best college. What do you think of his choice?

The Harder Right

1. Jason "never deliberately hurt anyone and what laws he broke were negligible." Is this enough to have a clear conscience?

2. In Jason's first dream he has to decide between doing nothing and letting a dozen teenagers die or diverting the train that will now kill one person.

3. In making life and death decisions, does it matter who the people are who will die? Does it matter what they are doing or why they are there? What other factors may go into making this decision?

4. Jason is changed by 9/11. He says that his non-violence had been "a rationalization for his cowardice." Do you agree? Do you think his change was for the better?

5. Despite the army's encouragement for him to become an officer, Jason rejects the invitation. He says he wants "no part of making decisions that affected the lives of others." Is there an obligation to assume responsibility when you have the ability? Is Jason suggesting that he simply wants to follow orders?

6. Jason asks himself how you decide when there is a conflict between orders given and ethical principles. What is your answer?

7. Jason comes to the conclusion that "minimizing casualties was the right thing to do." Do you think this is a good moral precept?

8. "Killing was sometimes a necessary evil," Jason believes. Do you agree? Under what conditions is killing moral?

9. Do you think Jason would make a different decision if the herders were boys or men?

10. The West Point Cadet Prayer says, "The essence of duty is acting in the absence of orders or direction from others, based on

an inner sense of what is morally and professionally right." On what basis does Jason make his decision to let the girls go?